A MEDIUM FATE

THE HAUNTED LIFE MYSTERY SERIES

LYNN CAHOON

A Medium Fate
The Haunted Life Cozy Mystery Series
Lynn Cahoon

DEDICATION

To Mary Burton who invited me to write for a SINC anthology and started me thinking about Eddie and her new life.

ACKNOWLEDGMENTS

This novella started as a short story call Casey's Treasures and was originally published in a much shorter format in DEADLY SOUTHERN CHARM. Eddie's story has been expanded in this and additional novellas coming in late 2022 and in 2023.

1

Timing is everything. It's a lesson I learned early in my life, especially when Dad was training me to do magic tricks. It's all about the timing. Even in conversations, you must have your timing right. Have you ever tried to input a comment into an ongoing conversation with two other people? I always wait for the right spot to say something when both of the other people have taken a breath. But by then my comment doesn't even make sense. Or worse, someone else has already said what I was planning on saying. Meetings are hell for me. I wind up looking like one of those hula dolls in the back of old cars. Just nodding away at everything someone else has already said but I'd thought about earlier.

Needless to say, meetings aren't the best part of any job. Maybe in anyone's job. However, I have the rare fortune to be in a position where my boss, Mr. Henry's meetings are actually the worst part of my job. Or anyone who works for Seattle Designs. Besides, of course, Mr. Henry.

It won't come as a surprise now when I tell you that every time Mr. Henry calls a team meeting at the local home design company, half the office disappears, citing their urgent need to be somewhere else. Anywhere else. Today, I got caught up on the phone with a supplier who still didn't have the light fixtures he'd promised for my client last month. I didn't see the mass exodus that started out of the cubical hell section where I sit. Worse, I didn't check my email for the impromptu announcement until it was too late.

I should explain that in order to get out of the office either through the stairs or the elevators, I have to walk by the main conference room. The walls were glass. And everyone, including Mr. Henry could see me leaving the building. So instead of an early lunch at eleven o'clock, I grabbed my cell phone, a notebook, and pen and joined the other laggards in the all-staff meeting. Which really wasn't even a quorum of the staff. I didn't know exactly what number that would be, but I heard it when I was watching a movie last night. And I knew it wasn't ten people.

"Miss Cayce? Are there any more stragglers in your section?" Mr. Henry growled at me as if I was the one that had made the rest of the team scatter.

"No sir, I was the last one. I was just finishing a call with a prospective client." I lied as I slipped into a chair near the doorway. That's me, Eddie Cayce. Junior level designer for the top interior design company in town. Probably in Washington state. Seattle Designs was the place I'd always dreamed of working during my graduate degree, until I'd gotten the job. Now I wondered why anyone with any creative bone in their body would work here. And please, no jokes about my name. My mom claimed I was a distant relative to the magician, but his powers and abilities with sleight of hand didn't pass on to me. Or at least, not when I was trying to stay out of meetings.

Mr. Henry harumphed and pointed to the door. "Well, you might as well close the door so we can get started. I'll send out an email to the rest of the crew with the details of the new copying procedure."

OMG. I froze my face into a polite smile, then stood up to close the door. I wondered if he'd even notice me if I made a run for it, but then again, I'd left my cell on the table. I was waiting for a call from my brother. Grandma Andrews wasn't doing well and I needed to plan my trip back home carefully since I was limited on vacation and the company frowned on employees taking unpaid leave.

Shutting the door, I sat down and tried to watch the forty-five minute presentation on using the new copiers. Which if I remembered right, had been the exact same presentation I'd watched during my week of orientation. Working for a corporation didn't allow for much individuality, but the benefits were better than the startup I'd worked for when I'd graduated from my master's in interior design and business program.

As the video played, I made a shopping list for the week. Cooking for one wasn't my strongest skill. David is out of town on a business trip this week. He's my almost fiancé. The ring is already in the box in his top drawer. I found it when I visited his apartment last week on a scouting trip as we were planning on moving in together. He wants to keep his apartment, but mine is more practical. And has more room. So I measured the apartment and the rooms to prove my theory. And did a little snooping.

David's apartment did have a killer view of the Seattle skyline and a balcony that he never uses. The con for my list is it costs twice as much as mine. Sitting in the meeting, I tried to imagine sharing an apartment, a life with David. My vision turned to him on an airplane, taking a rum and Coke from the stewardess and handing the drink to his seatmate. Seeing her through David's eyes, I could hear the thoughts going through his head. The girl was a knockout. Blonde hair, green eyes, and a doe like expression that just screamed *Take care of me.*

Okay, so I have at least one thing in common with my name sake. I can read minds. If I'm connected to the people or if the thought is directed at me. Like the message behind the look Mr. Henry was giving me right now.

I shook the vision away and tried to pay attention to the video. Watching people from afar didn't give the whole picture. Add in the fact that I could only see in sections that ran less than a minute of time. Some power, right? The glimpses I'd seen in the past had gotten me in more than a few jams, and, if I was honest, out of more uncomfortable situations. It's kind of like seeing into the future. So when I was single and saw a vision of the cute guy I'd just met at the bar getting a little too handsy, I would end the conversation before it got too far. Prejudging people may not be fair, but it's what I was given to work with.

Finally, the video ended but before we could leave, we had to take a test over the material we'd just watched. Good thing he didn't say we had to pass the test. I flew through most of the questions, only pausing at the one that asked who would replace the toner. The real answer was the next person who used the machine or tried to use the machine. If you could walk away undetected and not have to fix the machine, it was a win in the office Olympic games. I saw it like a bingo card. The big square in the middle was a free box. Days I hit bingo before noon, those were the good days. Mr. Henry's correct answer was whoever saw the problem first. Like that would happen.

Before I could finish the test, another vision blurred the outside world. In the vision, my phone rang and it was my brother, Nic with bad news. I'd waited too long. Not wanting to take this call surrounded by people, I quickly marked answers, not seeing the questions through the tears building in my eyes. My phone rang it's cheery tone and I stood and handed the paper to Mr. Henry who was monitoring at the door. "I've got to go."

"Miss Cayce!" Mr. Henry stepped in front of me, blocking my exit.

I willed the tears not to fall. "What? What now?"

He shook the paper in front of me. "You didn't put your name on the test. How do I know you were even here?"

"Besides seeing me and us having this conversation?" I ripped the paper out of his hands and using the wall as a flat surface, scribbled my name on the top. I shoved it back at him. My phone stopped ringing. "There. Now I've got to leave so move out of the way, or I'll move you."

Shocked, Mr. Henry stepped out of the doorway, and I hurried into the hall and found the first restroom. It was for the senior designers, but it had a door and a lock and a chair so I could sit and compose myself before I called. I sank into the chair and stared into the large vanity mirror that stared back at me.

Before I could call Nic, the phone rang. I answered, "I should have come last week."

"We didn't know she was this sick last week." Nic responded, trying to sooth my anxiety. "So you know."

"Tell me anyway. I can still hope I'm wrong." I set the phone on my lap and listened to his version of the story of how my grandmother, the woman I'd loved more in this life than anyone else, except maybe Nic, had left this world.

After he'd told me everything, he gave me the time and date of the memorial. "Eddie, I'd understand if you can't come. I just think you should have the option."

"I need to check with work. And talk to David. But I'll be there soon for at least a few days. I'll call as soon as I have plans." I took tissues out of a box on the vanity as the doorknob rattled. "Occupied."

"Sorry." A woman's voice called back.

It sounded like Erica from accounting, but I couldn't be certain. The blood was rushing in my ears muting anything I heard after Nic told me that Grandma Andrews had passed quietly in her sleep last night.

"Eddie, are you okay? Say something, you're worrying me." Nic's voice sounded warm and comforting. "Eddie?"

I took a breath. "I'm here. I just can't believe she's gone."

"I know. Just get here when you can. If you can't make it, the family will understand. I know you're busy with the job and, well, David. When's he going to pop the question? I'd feel better if I knew you had someone in Seattle looking out for you." Nic prodded.

"I have someone looking out for me. Me." I almost continued my rant about being independent, then I heard him laughing. "No fair trying to get me to feel better."

"She wouldn't want you to be sad, Eddie. She lived a long, good life." Nic murmured something I couldn't hear. "Look, I've got to go.

Let me know if you need picked up at the airport. I could send the company jet for you."

"I'll be fine. Let me clear up some things here first." I said good-bye, then dialed a new number. No one answered. I glanced at my watch. David should be at the hotel by now. I left a short message asking him to give me a call as soon as possible. I set the phone down on the vanity and checked my makeup. It was a total mess, but if I wanted to impersonate a racoon, I had the look down.

My vision wavered and instead of seeing my racoon eyes, I saw the inside of a bar, dark wood on the walls. The large bar had a mirror behind the bottles, making the liquor sparkle in the dim light. David sat at the bar, drinking a whiskey. As the phone beeped with my message, he looked at the display, then turned off his phone, tucking it into his jacket pocket. The woman from the plane came into the bar and sat next to him. He'd made a friend. Then as I watched, he leaned over and kissed her. A knife jabbed into my belly. He wasn't on a business trip. Or maybe it was, but it was also more than that. He was involved with this woman. An affair. I barely made it to the toilet before my morning smoothie came up.

I'd told Nic I had things to settle here before I could go home. I hadn't realized that ending a relationship would be on my to do list. There was no reason to stay here now. David and the job had been my main reason for building a life here in Seattle. Now, I didn't know.

I went to my cubicle and got my purse. I stopped at Mr. Henry's assistant's desk. "Sorry, I'm not feeling well. I need to go home."

"Oh, no." The older woman dropped her voice. "Did you get a visit from your Aunt Flo?"

"What?" My face heated as I got her meaning. "No, I mean, yes. That's what's happening."

"You poor girl. Put a heating pad against your tummy. It will help." She leaned closer. "He'll never know you're gone. Don't worry about it."

As I walked out, I wondered how long it would take to pack the stuff David had left at the apartment. I'd drop it off at his building on my way out of town. I could send Mr. Henry a resignation letter via email. There was nothing in my office desk I needed. Or wanted. Maybe I'd explain how the movie was just the last straw. That my creative juices were being stilted. It would be easier on the people I'd left if no one ever had to watch a video on using a copier ever again.

I could at least do that for my peers.

2

My plane landed in New Orleans just before three in the afternoon. I felt totally wiped. I'd been up since I'd talked to Nic with just a few cat naps in between. I'd slept a little on the plane, but the guy next to me kept trying to chat. Or he had to get up and pee every ten minutes.

I'd had a lot to get done. My apartment was boxed up, waiting for movers to come in next week. My landlord had gratefully let me out of my lease since rental prices had soared since I'd signed. David's stuff was with his building's super with a note explaining why I was breaking up with him. I included a description of the blonde. Just in case he was confused.

I'd filed a change of address with the post office. Since I'd never switched banks when I'd moved away for college, I was about done with my to do list. Maybe packing up and moving back home was an overreaction to David's cheating, but it wasn't just my relationship problems that was driving me to pick up my life and start over. My job was less than fulfilling. My heart was broken from the loss of my grandmother. All I could think of was how badly I needed to be home.

Nic must have found my travel plans because a driver waited near the baggage claim with a placard with my name on it. I adjusted my tote on my shoulder and stopped in front of the older man. "I'm Eddie."

"Why of course you are. You're the spitting image of your mother. I bet you get told that all the time. I guess you don't remember me, I'm Trenton. I've worked with your family for years, but you were so young back then. I drove you to the airport when you went off to college." He started walking toward the baggage claim. "I'm assuming you have luggage?"

"Sorry, of course I remember you. Two bags, I'm afraid they're pretty full. I needed enough to get through until my belongings arrive." Now I was oversharing. Trenton didn't care why my bags were heavy. Or, I assumed, that I was moving back. I was wrong on that point. He did care.

"Well, isn't that just perfect. The family will be so happy you're coming home. Do I take you to the compound first? Your brother and a few others are at the funeral home making final preparation. Your grandmother wanted a second line to take her from the church to the family vault." Trenton chatted about the funeral arrangements as we waited for my luggage.

"I need to make a stop at Hotel Monteleone to check in and drop off my luggage. I'm staying in town. Then you can take me to the compound. I need to see Nic. Do you mind driving me back into town tonight? If it's too much, I can get a rental." I needed to stay in town. The hotel would help me adjust by giving me a break from my Seattle life to my new life in New Orleans. Besides, something was brewing in my head about a new business. I didn't know what or why but staying in town was important but it was. My gut told me that.

"Of course, we can make the stop, but are you sure? You still have a room at the main house. I'll get you a car out of the garage to use until you make other arrangements. There's no need for a rental. We have too many cars just sitting now adays. But you look beat. I'll drive you back to the hotel tonight if that's what you want. I'll leave a car at the hotel for your use first thing in the morning." Trenton grabbed the luggage I pointed out and put them on a cart. Then he nodded to the exit. "We're that way."

"I need to stay in town. At least for a while." My head hurt from the lack of sleep and all I wanted to do was curl up on a bed and sleep. As much as I needed sleep, I needed to see my brother more. When I got into the back seat, I texted him. I'LL BE AT THE COMPOUND WHEN YOU'RE DONE. CAN I EAT DINNER WITH YOU?

The answering text came fast, like he'd been waiting. WE'RE ON OUR WAY BACK NOW. DINNER'S AT SIX.

I closed my eyes and for the first time in days, I fell into a sleep that didn't have dreams or nightmares. The next thing I knew, Trenton was gently shaking my shoulder. I wiped a line of drool from my chin. Not my best look. "I'm awake. I'll go check in and be right back."

"Miss Eddie, we're at the compound, not at the hotel. I already took care of checking you in. You were sleeping so hard I didn't want to bother you." He reached into his pocket. "I got your keys and put the room on the company card. You're all set."

I'd forgotten how easy it was to live here. Everyone took care of me. That had been the one reason I hadn't come home after college. I needed to know that I could do it on my own. But tonight, I was too tired to fight for my independence. Tonight, I wanted a meal, to talk with Nic and then my bed. Maybe not in that order. I might sleep for days.

Moving through the house to my old bedroom, I didn't see anyone. I still had a couple of hours before dinner. As soon as I opened the door to my old room, I kicked off my shoes and fell on the bed. Pulling a quilt up over me, I fell asleep.

I woke to the darkened room. Someone sat on the bed next to me. She ran her hand over my hair and made soothing noises. The room smelled like roses, the scent Grandma Andrews always wore. I blinked and no one was there. Sitting up, I rolled my shoulders. I should have expected a visit from my grandmother. Even dead, she wouldn't have missed the chance to welcome me home.

I picked up my tote where I'd dropped it next to the bed. I had stashed makeup, toiletries, and a change of clothes. I'd known that I'd be short on time when I got here. Being prepared was vital to making a proper showing in this family. The aunts and uncles would be at the table tonight. I'd get away with jeans and a nice shirt, but not the yoga pants and oversized tee I'd traveled in.

After I was ready, I checked my phone. Ten messages from David. I opened the phone app and listened as his messages went from confused, to angry, to crying. He admitted he'd been having an affair, but the trip was the first time they'd slept together. He promised. He begged me to call him and explain why I wasn't in our apartment anymore.

I deleted all ten messages. I might call in a few months to tell him where I was, but for now, I had a life to rebuild. Without worrying about David's feelings. Or getting sucked up by my family and their wants and needs for me. Sometimes having money was a curse. Especially when it made change hard. I glanced around the room. A vase of fresh flowers sat on a dresser and the refrigerator by my desk was filled with my favorite snacks and sodas. I opened it and yes, they'd even updated the selection to my current favorites. I grabbed a sparkling water and cracked it open. I drank down most of the bottle, dehydrated from flying. The water helped me feel clearer, so I finished that one and grabbed another to take to dinner with me. It was time to meet the family.

They were in the living room when I came downstairs. The aunts still called it the parlor. They looked up when I hit the last stair. Aunt Franny hurried to my side and enveloped me in a large, soft hug. Franny was a huge woman and she gave the bests hugs in town. Especially to a heart broken niece.

She held me out from her. Checking me over like I'd come home from a war. She was my mother's sister and had been the top fortune teller in the French District before she'd married one of her clients and became his rich widow a few years later. Now, she lived in an old mansion in the Garden district where she held teas and joined social organizations. "I'm glad to see you. Even if this is what had to happen to bring you home. Your brother says you might be staying? I'd love to introduce you to my Garden Club. Many of our members have suitable sons that you might consider if you're ready to settle down."

And there it was. The elephant in the room. My family thought I was too old to be unmarried. I'd probably moved into the Old Maid zone. Like there weren't men in Seattle. Well, they had that right, at least. The one man I'd thought about pledging my life to had been scum. Nic didn't get this kind of scrutiny about his love life, I bet. I closed my eyes and pushed away my first response which was snarky and cold. I opened them and smiled. "Aunt Franny, I'm way too busy right now figuring out what I'm going to do here in New Orleans to be dating. I'm sure I'll find the one sooner or later. You know soulmates can be a little tricky to find."

"Well, I'm just glad your home. You have plenty of time." She said, meaning she knew my time was running out. "Come in the parlor and let the rest of the family say hello."

Uncle Orrin and his wife, Gloria, were there. He and my father were brothers and had started the family business together. Now Orrin owned most of the river casinos in the area and Gloria was a homemaker. I didn't know exactly what Gloria did all day. Their son, Phillip, was in Boston in medical school to be a surgeon. Gloria showed me a picture of Phillip in his scrubs he'd snapped for them on the first day of residency last fall. She patted my arm. "Maybe Phillip knows some nice single doctors you could meet."

Before I could respond, Nic rescued me. A bad habit my older brother seemed to love to do. "We need to get to the table before everything gets cold. I'm sure Eddie will tell us all about what she's been doing in Seattle since she graduated head of her class in with an MFA focused on interior design and business, kicking my lowly MBA to the curb."

"Son, the stuff you learned from your MBA has taken Ardronic Family Corporation from the dark ages to where we're downright respectable. As long as you don't look too closely at our hands." Uncle Arthur chuckled. He held up his hands and twisted them back and forth. "It's all in the art of misdirection, right Nic?"

Uncle Arthur was my dad's other brother and the last of the aunts and uncles. He'd never married, and often said the job was his wife and mistress, although I thought he kept his personal life secret from everyone, even the family. Once, I saw him with a lovely Jamaican woman in a vision before he tuned in and looked right at me. He'd told me that he'd rather I stayed out of his head. Since that conversation within the vision, I'd never tried or even accidentally seen what was going on with my uncle. We both liked it better that way.

"Of course, Uncle Arthur, but we are respectable. At least that's what the books say." He led the group to the table and to my surprise, my brother sat me at one end of the table. He winked at me, then crossed over to the other end, sitting in the power position. The simple move announcing to our family that we weren't kids anymore. We were our parents' children and as such, the heads of the family. At least in this house.

Well, technically, Nic was the head of the family. And when he married, my seat would be taken by his wife. I'd become the spare heir in passing down power. My body tingled with a new source of power that confused me as it overwhelmed my senses. Maybe it was just being home again. My latent powers could be coming alive as I was near the magic well spring of our family tree. I hoped not. Even here in New Orleans, my plans were to live a normal life without magic. Or visions.

"That's not going to happen." Nic's words echoed silently in my head. I met his gaze and shook my head at him.

"Stay out of my thoughts, brother," I responded just as silently. Then I put up my walls and took a sip of the gumbo that had been set in front of me. Yes, moving home was going to be interesting.

Before I said my goodbyes and left to go back to the hotel, Nic pulled me aside into his home office. "The funeral is tomorrow. I'll have Trenton pick you up on our way there. Please don't argue. I'd like us to arrive together in a show of unity. There's been some discussion on maybe we should have a change of leadership at the company."

"Who? Not Uncle Arthur?" I felt shocked when Nic nodded. "He seemed like he was happy you took over when Dad died."

"He's just not happy with some of the changes I'm making. Like I said at dinner, I'm trying to make us respectable. That comes at a cost and with a level of fairness Arthur doesn't want to be held accountable to. I've come down on him several times this last year on falsifying employee work records and money from the shops." He leaned on the desk. "Look, I'm not asking you to get involved, but if you would at least look like you're supporting me, that would be great. You're probably wondering why I sat you at the end of the table with me."

"No, I understood the power play. You realize, once Esmeralda comes to her senses and moves back from California, she'll be taking that seat." I picked up a picture of him and his soulmate when they were kids at Carnival. "She was always so beautiful."

"She still is. She knows the power that she'll hold when she marries me. Honestly, I think that's why she hasn't said yes, yet. She keeps saying that town, South Cove, needs her." He took the picture from me and after looking at it, set it back in the exact place where I'd picked it up from. Nic liked his things orderly. "Anyway, that's why we need to be a unified team tomorrow. We'll leave the funeral, do the second line, then we're off to the will reading. We'll come back to the house for the reception after that."

"We're doing the will reading tomorrow. Isn't that soon?" I thought about the vision of Grandma Andrews I'd seen in my room.

"It's unorthodox yes, but it's in the will. Grandma set it up this way. I think she wants everyone to know exactly what she did before they start to bicker about her fortune." He gave her a hug. "You look beat. Go get some sleep and I'll see you tomorrow. Remember dress code is anything but black. You don't want to anger her spirit."

"I have a dark blue dress that will work. It will make me feel better about not wearing black and still meet Grandma's request." I touched my neck where the silver locket with her and Granddad Andrew's picture was set. She'd given it to me just before I'd left for college. She asked me to keep them close. And I had. "I'm going to miss her."

"I know." He reached out and touched a finger to the locket.

A knock sounded, then the door opened. Trenton poked his head inside the room. "Whenever you're ready, miss."

WITH THE FUNERAL over and the second line completed, I was back in the limo with Nic. Trenton was at the wheel, driving us to the lawyers office. I'd seen my aunts and uncles leaving the gravesite as the attendees held us back, talking about how much our grandmother had meant to them. No one but us and Aunt Franny were technically related to the Andrews part of the family, but that didn't mean that they weren't expecting to be part of the will. I had a bad feeling they were going to be disappointed.

I kicked off my one pair of Jimmy Choo's and rubbed my feet. "I love these shoes but I'm not used to dressing up anymore. Even the design firm was more a Birkenstock place. Hopefully, my next endeavor will be as comfortable."

"Come work for me at the business. I could use the help keeping Uncle Arthur in line. I'll give you a cool VP title and your own office. And probably twice what you made at that design place." He was scrolling his phone, answering emails as we talked.

"Maybe." I said, but I really meant no way. I looked out the window as we passed through the Garden district toward downtown. LaFollette Cemetery was old but it was where the Andrews family vault was located so there was never any choice on where the burial would occur. LaFollette also was the home of a fictional vault of a popular vampire from a local author's book series.

"It wouldn't be that bad." Nic set his phone down. "I could use the help. I need someone in the office I can trust."

"Nic, I'm going to be honest here. Working in the family business is not what I want to do with my life. You know that. I'm thinking about opening a design studio or if I can afford it, buying an antiques business. It all depends on the inheritance. I've set aside the rest of what Mom and Dad left. It's my retirement and freedom account. For situations like this one." I turned my head to watch the grand houses pass by out the window.

"I'm sorry about David. I can't believe he did that to you." Nic's voice was low so hopefully Trenton didn't hear my private business. But being at home meant one thing, I had no private business. Everything was up for discussion.

"I really don't want to talk about him." I'd had to delete another set of messages this morning. I should have blocked his number when I left Seattle, but I guess I wanted to hear his explanation. But sorry I cheated wasn't really a why and neither was the I made a mistake phrase that he used in every message. I had been looking for a reason, but maybe there wasn't one. The affair had happened and now we were over. Case closed.

"It's not your fault," Nic added to my internal ramblings.

I didn't waste the time to even answer. I knew the issue had been David. At least I found out before I said I do.

The attorney's office was in a high rise building near the French Quarter. Palm trees lined the road and as we pulled into the building's underground parking, the temperature cooled. Trenton paused at the entrance and a doorman opened my door and held out his hand. I'd walked to most places in Seattle, including back and forth to work. This royal treatment was nice, but annoying.

The air inside the parking lot was hot and humid, but that changed as soon as we got into the lobby and into the elevator. Nic pushed the button for the fifteenth floor. Neither one of us talked on the way. I didn't have to make decisions today, but I did need to support my brother in his position. Holding my tongue was never my strength.

The lawyer was waiting for us as the elevator door opened. He reached out and shook Nic's hand, then reached for mine. "Ms. Cayce, I'm so sorry for your loss. I'm Michael Dean, your grandmother's attorney."

The fact he didn't call me Ms. Ardronic made me like him at once.

And the fact he looked like Santa Claus in a suit didn't hurt either. "Thank you so much, Mr. Dean. Grandma will be missed."

I wanted to say how sorry I was that I didn't come home sooner, but he didn't need my apology. I'd already told the ghost of my grandmother the same thing several times and had been forgiven each time. I was beating myself up for my own perverted pleasure. I took a breath, hoping to push the regret away. At least for now.

"We're in the conference room. Several of your relatives have already arrived. We've been waiting for you two before we began." He walked down the hall toward the conference room and Nic caught my gaze. He'd been right. The family had tried to get the lawyer to explain what they'd received from the estate before we'd arrived.

Now the fun could begin.

3

The conference room was filled with my aunts, uncles, and what appeared to be a lawyer for each of them. The lawyers were in black suits, everyone else wore bright colors except for me and Nic. We were in dark blue. I couldn't have worn canary yellow even if my grandmother's ghost had requested it. I mourned for her. I knew she hadn't wanted me or anyone to mourn, but there it was. I couldn't see a future where the world didn't include my grandmother. Nic held out a chair for me and I slipped into it, wanting nothing more than to fall into my bed at the hotel and sleep for a week. Okay, maybe a year.

"Are you okay?" Mr. Dean set a cup of coffee and chicory blend in front of me. "I'm having some pastries brought in, but maybe lunch would be better? You all probably haven't eaten. Yet."

I was about to say no, when Aunt Franny spoke up. "That would be nice. My niece came in from Seattle for the funeral and I'm sure she's feeling the jet lag still."

I took the coffee and met Nic's gaze. He shrugged. This time, it hadn't been him to step in and save me, but the effect was still the same. Everyone thought I needed taken care of. I had always been the baby of the family and treated as such. Which was one reason I chose a college as far away from my family as possible. The fact that most of them didn't like flying had made it a perfect place to find my own footing. Yet, I'd given up spending these last years with Grandma. I wasn't sure today that it had been the right decision. "Thank you, Mr. Dean. I'm sure my blood sugar is a little low."

Mr. Dean hit a button on the table and quietly spoke to someone. Then he nodded to his assistants who were standing by a table with a pile of folders. "The food will be right here. Will readings be quite a lengthy process, especially when my colleagues find a need to attend. I would hate to have anyone pass out due to hunger. Besides, your grandmother set up the catering before her passing."

Nic squeezed my hand. "Of course, she did. Grandma Andrews felt feeding people was the highest act of love you could show."

A woman in a black suit set a folder down in front of me. The clear front cover showed Grandma's name and the words, last will and testament with a date. I pointed to that and looked up at Mr. Dean. "She signed the will two weeks ago?"

"The will has been done since your grandfather died, but we've updated it at least annually due to changes in the beneficiaries. Like when your parents died, and then she called me a few weeks ago to review and make some final changes. I guess she had a feeling." Mr. Dean waved in more assistants who set platters of food on the table with small plates. In front of me was a plate that held a mixture of croissants, beignets, and fruit. Some of the croissants had been made into sandwiches with ham or sausage patties and melted cheese. My stomach grumbled and I took one of the sandwiches, one of the powdered sugar covered beignets and several cubes of fruit. I wouldn't be passing out just because I didn't eat. I could take care of myself.

One of the lawyers, I think he was with Uncle Arthur frowned. "The timing seems convenient."

"Are you saying she knew when she was going to die?" Mr. Dean focused on the man who was now looking at Uncle Arthur. "If so, we lost a powerful prognosticator. Of course, this is the Ardronic family."

The other lawyer shook his head and sipped his coffee, not willing to take on the fight. At least not there.

Nic took two of the croissant sandwiches and the rest of the family filled their plates. Only the lawyers seemed to have already eaten that morning as they were busy looking through the will documents.

Mr. Dean waited a bit for the food to start to be consumed and then started reading the will aloud. I wasn't paying attention until Nic kicked my shoe with his foot. I met his gaze and realized we were at the distribution of assets portion.

"To my daughter, Fanny, I leave my French Quarter condo and a sum of fifty thousand dollars for its upkeep. I also give her my ruby necklace that was given to me by my grandmother. I have left the necklace to my attorney to hold so she won't be confused on which item is actually hers."

I saw Franny flush. But she kept her mouth shut. One of the assistants picked up a jewelry box from the back table and set it down in front of her.

"To my grandson, Nic, I leave the family property outside of New Orleans, the rest of the belongings including furniture inside and on the property that I don't specifically bequest to someone else, and the trust with funds that has been set aside to manage the property." Mr. Dean handed Nic another folder. "This has the trust documents as well as a complete inventory of the property and the belongings. Your grandmother had Trenton do the inventory of the house and surrounding property. You are now the owner of, among other things, an old tractor that is in the barn on the outer field. Your grandmother was very excited to hear that the tractor hadn't been sold when your father stopped farming the land years ago."

"Grandma Andrews loved talking about the land and all the blessings it had given the family over the years." Nic took the folder and set it under the will folder. "Maybe I'll become a gentleman farmer in the future."

I squeezed his arm. "Grandma would love that. But I don't think it's in your blood."

He laughed and wiped at his eyes, "You're probably right there. I like my suits and shiny shoes too much."

The others gathered at the table chuckled quietly, but even I could feel the edge. Grandma's will hadn't discussed the bank accounts yet. Aunt Franny, who was quietly watching Nic and I, had been the only other person mentioned yet. The rest were all still expecting a windfall.

Mr. Dean returned to his seat. "There's just a little more. And to my granddaughter, Eddie Cayce, I leave the rest of my estate. Any accounts or coins or monetary amounts not otherwise bequeathed are to go to my dear Eddie. I hope you find that home can be a place of support and independence at the same time. Live your wildest dream, my dear."

Mr. Dean closed the folder.

"That's it?" Uncle Arthur demanded. "Just those three get all of her estate?"

Mr. Dean nodded. "There were a few gifts to charity that happened as soon as I was notified of her death per her request. She left fifty thousand to the animal shelter and the same amount to a local private school, New Orleans Academy, but the rest has been divided between the three blood decedents."

I thought he'd probably made that clarification for the other lawyers in the room. He walked over and handed me a folder. I looked up at him. "What's this?"

"That's a listing of the accounts and amounts of your inheritance. Before you leave, I'll have you sign the paperwork to switch over the bank accounts to your name. It will be with the bank your family has used, but of course, as soon as the process is complete, you can switch money over to whatever bank you want." Mr. Dean went and sat in his chair. He took a beignet from the platter in front of him and took a bite. Then he brushed the powdered sugar from his jacket. "I should have taken this off first. I always make a mess with these. Did anyone have any questions?"

"How much was the inheritance to Eddie?" Uncle Orrin asked Mr.

Dean. He was staring at me like I'd taken his favorite toy or something.

"That is privileged information and I'm not allowed to divulge it. Ms. Cayce can or she can choose not to answer either."

Now everyone was staring at me. I closed the listing that I'd only glanced at before. It was a few million from what I could tell, but some was in stocks, some in bonds. I would need some time to dig through what Grandma Andrews had left me to see what I actually had. But I knew one thing. It wasn't anyone's business but mine. "I haven't had time to review the listing yet."

"But about how much was it?" Aunt Gloria pressed me for an answer. "You can see the balances and add up numbers. You graduated from college for gosh sakes."

Now, they were insulting me. I hated being back home. I shut the folder and stared right at her. "I don't feel the need to tell you."

The room went quiet and then everyone, including the lawyers started talking at once. Nic squeezed my arm as a show of solidarity. Finally, Mr. Dean stood and banged what looked like a gavel on the table. The sound stopped the questions. "Sorry, I'm afraid our time here is up. There's another meeting in the conference room in five minutes. Mr. Ardronic and Ms. Cayce, please follow me to my office so we can get this paperwork filed."

"We will be asking a judge to put a hold on probate until the will is verified." Uncle Arthur's attorney stood.

"I've already talked to Judge Olden. He's waiting for your call. We expected a challenge, but I assure you, the will is valid." Mr. Dean nodded to his assistants. "Please give the attorneys a copy of the judge's contact information."

Mr. Dean stepped in between Nic and I and shepherded us out of the room. When we were in the hallway, he murmured, "Well, that went better than I'd expected."

I turned back and looked at the group of relatives huddled around their respective attorneys. "You were expecting that reaction? What's wrong with them? I can't believe they're even thinking about challenging the will."

"Your grandmother amassed a lot of money and probably certain assumptions were made over the years. Don't worry, the will is valid, the judge is aware of the special circumstances, and any challenges will be snuffed out quickly. Probate will be finished in a week or so." He opened a door. "This is my office. I'll set up the paperwork. It won't take much time, but it will be enough for my staff to get your relatives out of the building and the parking lot before you leave. I've installed security at the house as well, just in case."

"You think they'd just go in and take something?" Now I was worried.

Nic shook his head. "That's not going to happen. I think Grandma was afraid that they'd try to influence us to renounce our inheritance. That's one of the reasons I wanted you to stay at the compound instead of in town. I can assign a bodyguard for you there too. Besides, there's one more thing we need to talk about."

"I've got the papers on my desk along with more coffee or other drinks. If you want something else, just ask Carrie. I'll be here when you're ready." Mr. Dean held open the interior doors to his office. "I believe everything you need is set up. Your grandmother had very detailed notes."

Nic put his arm around me and led me to the office, shutting the door behind us. "Now, don't go crazy on me, but Grandma left you another inheritance."

"I don't understand." I turned back and looked at the closed door. "If there's something else, shouldn't the lawyer be giving it to me?"

Nic led me to a seat and nodded for me to take it. After I sat down, I prodded him for an answer. "Seriously, you're scaring me."

He sat across from me and took a paint brush and dipped it into a jar he'd just opened. Then he took my left hand and used the brush to draw a symbol on my hand. The smell hit me before I could react. Blood.

The energy flowed through me as I stared at the glowing symbol. Grandma Andrews had left me her gifts. As one of two female descendants, the power would have gone to me or to Aunt Franny. I'd hoped my aunt had mended her issues with Grandma before her death, but based on the symbol on my hand, that hadn't happened. After the initial rush of power, I let my gaze drift upward toward Nic. "I didn't want this."

"I don't think you had a choice. She'd left you the power. This," he waved at the blood and the symbol, is just the physical transfer. This way, you are in control. If we hadn't done this, the power would have chosen when and where to show up. You know the rules. It's passed after the owner is buried. And to the female descendent of that person's choosing. The only way you could have said no was to die. Honestly, I'm not ready to lose my only sibling over an inability to accept her powers."

"She should have given it to Aunt Franny." Tears threatened to fall, but I turned my head and stood, taking the vial of blood to the small bathroom next to the office. I had never been in this office before, but I'd known where the door to the bathroom was. Because my grandmother had been here. I knew what she'd known. Which meant I knew why she hadn't given it to Aunt Franny. After I'd dumped the blood and washed out the vial, I came back into the office. I looked at my brother for confirmation of the answer that had just been provided to me. "Aunt Franny used a love spell on her last husband? Are you kidding me?"

Nic grinned. "I guess the memories have transferred to you. Yes, that's the story Grandma Andrews told me when she told me about the inheritance. I'd asked her the same questions. I knew you were happy in your Seattle life and didn't want to come back."

"Well, let's just say I was in denial in my Seattle life. Happy being an idiot." I held up my hand, warding off the questions about my relationship with David. Or the support. "It's over, I don't want to talk about it. What I want to do is start a new life here. I guess I've got the funding to start or buy a business now. How much of a problem are the aunts and uncles going to be? Do I need to hold off spending some of that money?"

Nic wrapped the empty vial and the small paintbrush in a white handkerchief and tucked it in his pocket. "I'll have Trenton start a fire in the living room when I get home. This will be gone before nightfall. It's tradition."

"Thanks, I know you'll handle it. I trust you." I glanced around the desk making sure Grandma's blood hadn't leaked or dropped anywhere. "But what about the money?"

"That question is for our attorney. I'll let him know we're ready." He went to the door to get Mr. Dean, as I sat back down. The food had helped me not pass out when the ceremony was performed, but now I was starving. A plate full of croissants sat on Mr. Dean's desk, and I took one and ripped open to eat the buttery insides. Then I ate another.

I glanced at my hand where Nic had drawn the family symbol, but the blood was gone. Instead, I now had a cute tattoo of a lion. Our family mascot. Family lore said our blood line was out of Romania, part of the roving bands of gypsies that caravanned around Europe. I hadn't ever traced our history, but now, with so much in my head, memories from one practitioner to the next, lifetime after lifetime maybe I'd write it down in case I had a daughter. Or worse, in case I didn't.

"Everything taken care of then?" Mr. Dean asked as he studied me. I wasn't sure what he was looking for, maybe a second head, but I felt the same as I had before we'd come into his office. Maybe a tad less sad since I could feel Grandma's presence in the back of my mind. The locket had kept her and Grandpa near my heart, but this level of connection felt like she was standing behind me.

"Yes, we're done. However, Eddie and I would like to know about the inheritance process. Do you think the relatives have a chance at breaking the will?" Nic sat next to me.

Mr. Dean crossed the room and sat at his desk. I got the feeling he was using it as a shield against me. He knew the power we, or I guess, I now held. And it scared him. Even though he'd been the family lawyer for years. And before that, his father had been our attorney. And his grandfather. When he retired, the family attorney role would pass to the next generation. It was in our contract with the Dean family. They were well compensated for their loyalty. I didn't want him to be frightened of any of us. Unless you counted Uncle Arthur. He was scary.

A smile crossed Nic's face and I realized he'd been listening to my thoughts. I broke the connection and put up a wall. Something I needed to do every morning for the rest of my life. A wall to protect my thoughts as well as those of my ancestors I'd just been given.

I refocused on what Mr. Dean was saying.

"The judge has already reviewed the will and the facts in the case. There's no reason to break the will or change the inheritance. They can sue, but that won't cost you anything. We'll get our money from the losing side and believe me, they will lose. Your grandfather's will was contested by your uncle a few years ago when everything went to your grandmother except for the business which went to Nic. He lost then. He'll lose again. And, they had more ammunition back then since your uncle worked in the business for so many years." He set a packet of papers in front of each of us. "Time to sign and make this all legal. Then, Ms. Cayce, you can spend the money anyway you want to."

I started to sign. Without looking up, I said, "I'm going to buy an antique shop. Do you know any brokers that specialize in that type of business? I'd love to acquire one on Royal if possible."

He drummed his fingers on the desk. Then he opened a drawer and pulled out a card. He slid it across the desk toward her. "I don't know any that are currently for sale, but I hear rumors. Call Daniella. She's the best in town. She'll find you a shop."

4

Two weeks later, I found myself sitting at Café Du Monde waiting for Danielle LaCrosse once again. I was beginning to think it might be months, maybe years, before the right shop came available at a price I wanted to pay. Yes, I had the money to buy the two overpriced shops I'd seen so far, but that was the problem. People in the New Orleans area saw my name and added a couple of zeros to the price before I walked in the door. And that was with me using my grandmother's maiden name. The Ardronic/Cayce name dripped power and money in this town. Unfortunately, I wasn't ready to spend money like my aunts and uncles did. Sue me for being practical.

And there was the little thing about accepting Grandma's Andrew's powers. Now, everywhere I went, a ghost wanted to chat or file a grievance about their afterlife. Like I could control the fact that the current residents of a local French Quarter building were tearing out the wallpaper and painting the living area black. Design wise, I agreed with the ghost I'd met on yesterday's walk on the lack of class for the change. Practically, there was nothing I could do to make the new, living, owners' change their mind. Except drop off a card with my design company website and phone number.

I informed the ghost that if they called, I would try to guide them away from the changes, but that was all I could do. The woman had disappeared in a huff and I hadn't received a call from the misguided homeowners.

Today, a ghost sat next to me at my table while I waited for Danielle to arrive. I was trying to read as I let my coffee cool from the just short of surface of the sun temperature the café served it to almost drinkable. The ghost was enjoying the smells and trying to get me to order beignets.

"Just one." The older woman in a *I Love Nola* t-shirt suggested. She'd told me her name was Helen and she'd been hanging around the café for the last year. "I didn't even get to eat one when Frank and I came here on vacation. I had a heart attack before the food was even served."

I looked up from the book, a thriller from an author I loved. "If the waitress comes by before Danielle gets here, I'll order one. But please, let me read."

She clapped her hands in joy and the breeze from her excitement blew a napkin off my table and onto the next table crowded nearby. The man at the table grabbed it and handed it back to me. "That's the first puff of wind I've felt since I sat down in this tent."

"Thanks, it was probably from the fans." I took the napkin and pointed upward to the fans that were slowly circulating but not making much of an effort to cool down the overcrowded tent.

He looked upward and frowned, but then nodded and went back to chatting with the woman next to him.

I frowned at my table companion, and she laughed. "Sorry, I forget that not everyone can see me. How come you can see me? Are you related to Marie LaBoo?" The ghost continued to chatter. "I did get to see her tomb in St Louis Cemetery #1. We went there the morning I died. Maybe I got heat stroke."

"It's Marie Laveau you're thinking of. According to legend, she was the voodoo queen of New Orleans in the 1800's. She was also an herbalist and midwife. Basically, she served as the local doctor of the times, but everyone puts supernatural powers on things they don't understand. Especially when a woman is healing sick people." I pointed to my earbud as the man from the other table stared at me for talking to myself. He nodded and smiled. At least with modern technology I didn't look like I was talking to voices when I got into a public discussion with a ghost.

Danielle arrived before the waitress much to Helen's dismay. I tucked the book away and picked up my still hot cup of coffee and went to meet her. "I'm ready if you are."

The business consultant gave me a quick hug and nodded to my cup. "The last time I had coffee here, I burned my tongue and couldn't taste anything for three days."

"It's still hot and I've been here since nine." Which had been our agreed upon meeting time. Now it was twenty minutes later. Things moved slower in the South. We had ten minutes to walk to the antique shop.

"I called Matty Goldstein and told him we might be a little late. He's fine with it. Of course, I need to warn you. He puts the place up for sale every few years and gets offers, but he never sells. I think he uses the offers to support his bank financing. I hear the place is overextended on its loans. So maybe this time, he really wants to sell. But I wouldn't bet on it." Danielle walked on the sidewalk and through the crowd of tourists moving toward Jackson Square. "We can walk faster to the shop than try to find a cab."

"It's crowded today." I dodged a man handing out flyers for one of the Bourbon Street bars. "I thought weekends were the busy time down here."

"Every day's busy anymore. I swear, we have more tourists every year. Have you thought about looking at shops in the Garden District instead? I know a few out there that are willing to entertain an offer." We were paused at a light, and she looked at me hopefully.

"It's a possibility. I wanted to be on Royal Street. But I'm not willing to pay extra just because I'm desperate." I glanced at my watch again. We were two minutes late now and still a few blocks away from the shop.

A woman in a flowered dress and several plastic bead necklaces walked through the crosswalk and the car that was driving past us. I blinked as I saw her reemerge on the other side and smile at me. This power was going to take some time to get used to, that was for sure. Maybe setting up a shop away from the high tourist traffic might not be a bad idea. Antique shoppers loved small quaint shops in beautiful neighborhoods. If I could find the right property, it might just be a better location.

The only problem was I had my heart set on a French Quarter setting.

As we got closer to Bourbon Street, the tourist traffic slowed. People must be sleeping in after a night at the bars. We turned onto Royal and went past my favorite dinner place, The Court of Two Sisters. Honestly, we could have met at my hotel and been closer to the shop, but Danielle had called to confirm the appointment after I'd already left to walk around. I looked behind me and spotted the bodyguard Nic had assigned me. I'd thought I'd lost him on my walk to the coffee shop, but no such luck.

He, and his relief, always wore a black suit with black sunglasses. He looked like a cast member of The Men in Black. And somehow, it didn't look weird in the mix of tourist clothes and feather boas. The name he'd given me to call him was Bubba. He didn't match the image that came up with the name. I knew it wasn't his real name. He was probably an Edward or a Michael or a Thomas. I'd learned as a child from our own security team at the compound that most of the time, our guys didn't give out their real names, just a code name they were assigned when they were hired. I'm sure his employer had gotten a good joke out of calling the blond, blue-eyed tall slim man that was now two people behind me, Bubba.

I waved at him as we crossed over another street. He furrowed his eyebrows. Apparently, he didn't want people to know he was following me. Or he was mad at how I'd tried to ditch him earlier. I expected a call from Nic anytime telling me to stop being childish.

As we got closer to the building, my heart started to race. Hopefully Matty truly wanted to sell this time because I knew the multi-level building held floors crowded with furniture, antiques, and, if rumors were true, a few Egyptian artifacts with questionable papers. I wanted the building, the contents, and the location.

Danielle was already on the next showing telling me about a quaint little store in the middle of the Garden District near Lafayette Cemetery #1 and Commander's Palace. "Shall I set up a visit tomorrow? We can ride the street cars out there if you'd like. I'll treat you to lunch."

"Let's see how today goes, but I'm willing to look." I groaned inwardly. If she knew I was considering a different location, she might not be as intense on getting me something in the French Quarter. My brother's voice echoed in my head, *you're too nice and stop ditching Bubba.*

In response, I tightened my walls to keep him out. That's what nice does, I responded as I finished the wall in my head. I heard a chuckle on the other side. My brother's connection with me was getting stronger the longer I stayed in New Orleans. One of the reasons I'd left in the first place was so I didn't have to worry about who was listening into my thoughts. Now, I needed to find a way to keep him out, even if we were standing side by side. A niggle in the back of my mind told me that one of my ancestors memories had a solution, but I'd have to deal with it later.

I stared up at the building. Goldstein's Antiques had a first level of big, showcase windows, then the tan building moved upward with only three windows on this side per floor that I could see. The buildings next to it were built close and I didn't think I could walk between them. So having windows on those sides was kind of useless. "I love this place."

"Well, don't love it too much. You know we're already behind the eight ball since your family is well known in the area and it's rumored you just came into an inheritance. A fact I'm ignoring and trying to convince others that it's just a rumor. Talk about your work in Seattle. Why you want to own an antique store. And maybe how much you love the area. Just don't be too sold on the building going in. We need some sort of negotiation leverage to have a ghost of a chance with Matty."

A passing by ghost giggled at the word choice and nodded at me. Then she disappeared into the building next door.

I nodded and followed her into the antique store, trying not to follow my gaze and gush over the pieces crowded into the first floor. If I got this place, I'd clear it and then reset little vignettes. I could see that table set with the china stashed over by the window with the over-the-top chandelier hanging above. And the monkey light on a fake wall with over the top wallpaper. I tried to stop resetting the pieces as Danielle asked the salesman who'd come to greet us where we could find Matty.

"He's in his office on the second floor." The man frowned as he looked at us. His name tag said his name was Mark and he was happy to help, but he didn't look too happy. "Is he expecting you?"

"Yes. Point us to the elevator and we'll go up." Danielle said as a customer came in and started gushing over the monkey lamp. "That way you can help your customer."

The frown deepened, but he pointed to the side wall. "It's over there, behind the customer service sign. I'll call him and let him know you're coming."

I watched as he pulled his cellphone out of his pants and dialed while walking toward the new arrival. That man had an attitude and if I got to buy the place, he'd be one of the first to go. Maybe it was the lack of food that was making me grumpy. I should have gotten that beignet that Helen wanted to enjoy. I saw Bubba standing guard outside, looking through the window at me. I wondered if he'd freak out when we got on the elevator, but he knew I was looking for a store to buy. Maybe he'd treat me like an adult and let me work. It would be a nice change of pace after being home with my family for the last few weeks. Aunt Franny had called me every night for the last week, trying to set up time to chat. Or dinner. Or coffee. Or meet some nice son of a friend. I couldn't even think about the horror of a dinner with a guy who my aunt was trying to matchmake with me.

I pushed the up button, there was also a down, which told me the place had a basement as well. Hopefully nothing important was down there since the area had problems with flooding and hurricanes.

When the door opened on the second floor, we stepped into a warehouse filled with boxes and furniture and items. "That weasel gave us the wrong floor," Danielle grumped.

We went back into the elevator and pushed the button for the third floor. This time when the doors opened, a sign pointed left toward offices and right to the employee break room.

I stepped out and turned left. "Maybe he meant to say third."

Danielle shook her head. "No, he was playing games with us. Which means Matty is too. This was probably a waste of time. Sorry to get your hopes up."

"It's worth a shot. Let's see what he really wants and see if I can go that high." I kept thinking about the dining room scene I'd imagined on the first floor. And now, I'd already seen several items on the second floor that should be front and center in those showroom windows. Matty wasn't taking advantage of what he owned.

"Okay, it's your time to waste, I guess." Danielle walked up to Matty's door and knocked.

"Come in," a deep, masculine voice responded. As we walked into the office, I saw that Matty Goldstein liked the finer things in life. The room was filled with items I would have had out to sell, not locked away in my office. The oriental rug itself was probably worth over ten thousand. And I didn't even want to price in my head the desk he was sitting at with a soda sitting by his computer. Without a coaster. I swallowed and fought my urge to go pick it up and put something, anything under it so it didn't ruin the finishing. Or the wood.

I let Danielle take the lead on the conversation. I focused instead on Matty Goldstein. His thoughts were jumbled all over the place. Danielle's sources had been right, Matty was bleeding money in the business. They weren't making a profit, and now, he wasn't going to be able to make his bank payments. The thought of foreclosure hung over him like a black balloon. He hadn't set up the business as a corporation or even an LLC. He was sole owner and proprietor of Goldstein's Antiques, and he was going to go down with the ship.

When Danielle introduced me and asked me to tell Matty why I was interested in buying the business, I laid it on thick, hitting all the sore spots I'd found while observing the man. "I love design. It's my passion and all I can think about when I see a place is how beautiful it would be with a few tweaks. Like your showroom. Customers are probably having trouble finding the items they want, so they leave and go somewhere else where it's less crowded and more focused on furniture for beautiful homes. I can set up the showroom so the place will continue to thrive, even when you're in Jamaica on your first holiday for what, five, ten years?"

"Ten," he admitted. "But you know how it is with a small business. It takes all your time."

"When you let it." I shook my head. "Look, I know you're probably not even interested in selling, but what if selling actually gave you a chance at a new life. A life you've been meaning to live since you took over the family business. We all have an expiration date. Do you want to experience yours in this beautiful office? Or on a yacht sailing the Mediterranean Sea? It's your choice."

Matty picked up his soda and finished it. Then he took his shirt sleeve and wiped up the moisture the can had left on the desk. "You make a good argument. Danielle has my asking price. If you're okay with that, I'll consider selling. I would like to see Greece."

He didn't add, before I die, but I could see the wheels turning in his head. I'd made my pitch and that was all I could do. I stood and thanked him for his time. Then Danielle, who was staring back and forth at the two of us like we were crazy stood as well. "Eddie and I will write up an offer and get it to you tomorrow."

"Sounds like a plan." He smiled and stood to shake our hands. When he reached out to me, he said, "I am so sorry about your grandmother. I knew her back when we were both young and foolish."

His terminology made me smile. "I've never known my grandmother to be either of those things, but I'd love to hear stories."

He clasped a second hand over mine. "Maybe the next time we meet we can have lunch and I'll tell my tales."

"Thank you for your sympathy and your time," I said as we started out of the office and back to the elevator. "I'm looking forward to talking soon."

As we rode the elevator down, Danielle blew out a breath. "Well, I hadn't expected that. Do you still want to see the Garden District property tomorrow?"

"Why not. Write up the offer, I'll sign it tomorrow and then we'll go look at another option, just in case he says no." I didn't think he would reject our offer. Maybe ask for more money which I'd have to consider before agreeing, but I thought he'd eventually accept. Looking at the Garden District property would give me an idea on what my competition would be. "I haven't been to the Commander's Palace in years."

As we walked toward my hotel where Danielle would catch a cab back to her office, I imagined all the things I could do with the first-floor showroom to bring in customers and local design houses. Danielle was talking about all the advantages of being located in the Garden District. She's already moved on, thinking that Matty Goldstein was going to say no.

I knew better. Goldstein Antiques was mine. Now all I had to do was sign the paperwork and write a check.

5

I'd brought the car since I'd had to be at the compound later today. Now, I sat outside the old brick building on Royal Street watching a sidewalk sleeper roll up his sleeping bag. It was clear the man had been sleeping huddled in the entry way of Goldstein Antiques. I pulled a ten out of my tote and climbed out of the SUV. The brick sidewalk still showed signs of the party crowd that reveled throughout the French Quarter until early this morning. How the guy actually slept on the hard concrete I didn't know and I didn't want to find out.

"I'm not doing nothing." The man mumbled as I moved toward the doorway. "You all are here way too early. Customers don't show up until after ten."

"Who else has been here?" I held out the bill, hoping the man would use it for a meal. He looked gaunt.

With a dirt caked hand, he grabbed the money without looking me in the face. "Just the guy."

I saw the moment he made the police cruiser slowly driving down the one-way street. He stuffed the bill into his pants and the sleeping bag into a small rollaway cart and took off in the opposite direction.

"So much for having a conversation with the locals." I waved at the officer inside the cruiser who was now watching me.

The joy and problems of running a business in the historic New Orleans neighborhood had just become my concern. Or had yesterday at two when I'd handed Matty Goldstein a check for the building and all the contents.

Now I owned an antique shop in the heart of the French Quarter I'd never been happier. A black Range Rover pulled up behind my car and I met my brother on the street in front of the shop.

Nic paused on the street, staring at the building. His dark hair was a touch too long and curled over his ears. His dark eyes took in the condition of the building, clearly not impressed. He reached down and picked up a red solo cup from the street. "This is what you get for your inheritance from Grandmother Andrews. Having buyer's remorse yet?"

"Not on your life, Nic. I'm looking forward to starting this new chapter." I thought about my recent move home. After settling in Seattle, I'd thought life would keep me far from my Louisiana roots. Instead, I was back. I dug the ring of keys Matty had handed over yesterday and grinned at my brother. "Want to see the inside?"

"Why not. My first appointment isn't until noon." Nic threw the cup into an overflowing trash can. "You'll need to hire someone to clean each morning before your customers arrive. And I don't want you staying late here. If we don't keep security on you, call me if you leave after dark and I'll send someone to follow you home."

"I found my way home for over ten years in Seattle all by myself. In fact, I've been doing it a lot since I turned thirty. Besides, for now, there's always Bubba." I waved at the man who sat in a black sedan across the street watching us. I fit the key into the lock. Nic hadn't needed to show up to help me open the building, but he loved treating me like a child. The door didn't move after I'd heard the lock engage. Why hadn't it opened? "That's weird."

Nic took the key from me and quickly opened the door. "You don't think it was left open, do you? Who else has keys to this old firetrap?"

"I don't know." The thought worried me as I pushed open the

door. The lights were already on, a detail I hadn't noticed in my haste to get inside. I paused just inside the doorway. "Hello? Is someone there?"

An older woman with her hair in a bun stepped out of a side room. She was dressed in a black pant suit. She peered at us. Probably sizing us up as potential buyers. I'd fallen short in her eyes as her gaze took in my clothes and canvas tote, but her face softened into a smile when she saw Nic's Rolex. She hadn't figured out we were related, probably because of my short and currently burgundy hair. Add in the fact Nic was five to six inches taller. We looked as different as night and day. "Good morning early birds. You're my first customers of the day. What can I help you find?"

"Who are you?" I asked, feeling Nic's elbow in my side.

The woman blinked but gained her composure quickly. "I'm Sarah Stiner. I'm sure if we don't have what you're looking for, I can find it. Who am I helping today?"

Nic stepped in between me and the woman. "My name is Nicolae Ardronic. This is my sister, Eddie Cayce. She purchased the building and the business yesterday from Mr. Goldstein. I take it you weren't informed of the change of ownership?"

The woman's eyes widened. "Matty, I mean, Mr. Goldstein sold the store?"

"Yes." I held up the ring of keys he'd give me. Then I heard a noise from the back. "Who else is here?"

Sarah shook her head. "No one. I open the store Mondays through Friday's exactly at eight. I don't work weekends. I just saw Matty yesterday. Why wouldn't he have told me?"

I was wondering the same thing but I was still worried about who else was in the building. "I heard something in the back. Are you sure there's no one else here?"

"That's probably Harry." Sarah sank into a nearby chair and put her head in her hands. "I've worked here for over ten years. What am I going to do now?"

"Who's Harry?" Nic put a hand on the woman's shoulder. "Can I get you a glass of water?"

Sarah nodded. "Thank you, that would be nice. There's a small breakroom at the back, past the accounting office. And Harry, well, he's the building ghost."

I met Nic's gaze. Of course, there was a ghost. The building was probably original to the founding of New Orleans. Every building had at least one story that the tourist trade used to build up business for the nightly ghost tours. "I'll go get the water."

"Eddie, be careful. She's not wrong." Nic glanced around the shop.

I tried not to roll my eyes in front of my brother. He'd been taught by our father the family fortunetelling business. I knew it more for the con than the connection to some so-called other side. Besides, with my new 'power' if there was someone here, I'd know. Nic was better with real people. He didn't have Grandma's extra shine.

I made my way to the door marked, Employees Only, and pushed my way through. Apparently, Matty Goldstein had been a little too excited about his big payoff to deal with his employees yesterday. Hopefully, I could get ahold of him today and have him break the news to the rest of the staff. I'd rather hire my own crew than take over ones that had been loyal to the aging dealer. But if I had to keep a few, I could work with that.

For not the first time, I wondered if coming home after the breakup had really been the best idea. There were other cities where I could have bought a failing antique business. Probably cheaper too. But I'd been drawn home. Now I had to deal with the consequences. At least here my 'power' wouldn't be looked on like a curse.

I passed by a small office and then pause at next. From the sign over the door, the break room was the next doorway. The sign on this door said, *Conference Room.* I pushed open the door and stood dumbstruck. A man sprawled face down on an oriental rug, stained crimson with blood. From the thinning hair and large size, I thought I'd found the man I'd handed a check to yesterday.

Matty Goldstein wasn't going to be telling his employees anything about the sale. He was dead.

~

"ARE you sure the building sale was completed?" The detective in a bad suit asked me for the third time. I sat in the employee break room, drinking coffee and going over the events that had led me to purchase the store for the last hour.

"I handed him a check. We signed the documents. The title company was filing all the paperwork. The sale was complete." I glanced over to where Nic sat, working on his phone. He'd cancelled his appointments for the day and now was waiting for me.

Bubba stood in the corner, hands behind his back, watching the door.

"Okay, we'll be in touch. The coroner has taken the body to the morgue and the crime scene guys have finished their work." The detective, Boone Charles, closed his notebook and handed me a card. "I've written down the items we took out of the conference room on the back. It's your receipt, although I don't think you're going to want that rug back."

"So you're done here? We can clean up and open?" I took the card and dropped it into my tote. I didn't want to sound insensitive, but on the other hand, I'd begun to look at the company's books while we waited for the police to finish. We needed sales to keep going.

"Not today you're not." Nic stood by my side and handed the detective his own card. "Thank you for being so quick on this, Detective Charles. If you need to talk to my sister, she'll be staying at my house tonight."

The man stood and shook Nic's hand. Then he looked down at me. "Sorry that your first day back turned into such a disaster."

"It's not my first day back, I've been here for a few weeks. I'm staying at the Monteleone." I felt like I was babbling. Looking at my brother, I could see the concern in his eyes. "But I guess not tonight."

Boone stepped toward the door. "It's still a shame."

After we were alone, Nic turned me toward him. Bubba stood outside the door. "Are you sure you're, okay? You found a dead body."

"Maybe in shock a little. Man, this is not how I planned to spend the day. I was going to pull up the inventory list and go through it all, making notes on where and what condition everything was in." I followed him out to the hallway, pausing at the elevator. "Hey, can we at least look for his records? These sales records I found in the business manager's office are making me a little nervous. According to this, the store hasn't had a sale over two hundred dollars in over a month."

Nic glanced at his watch. "Of course. I've had your car taken to the compound. Annamae's making dinner for us. Bubba, stay on this floor and watch the front door, please."

Which was code that I didn't have much time. Nic had learned the art of speaking without being direct from our father. It drove me crazy. *Say what you mean and mean what you say.* That had been Mom's motto for years.

Fifteen minutes later, we'd gone through the office without finding much of anything. Nic pointed to an empty cord. "Maybe the police took his electronics."

I sighed and gave up. "I guess so. I'll look closer tomorrow when I come in."

Passing by the second office, I paused. I had a strong feeling I needed to open the door. Reason number four hundred and five that I shouldn't have come home. My own psychic powers were coming back after I'd been able to ignore their existence for years. I saw Nic felt the same draw to the room. I put my hand on the knob. "Might as well check it out."

A Queen Anne desk set in the middle of the room. A laptop was on the top, looking out of place. As I crossed the room, I also saw an envelope with my name scrawled on the front. I opened it and read the enclosed letter. "It's from Matty. He loaded all the records on the laptop for me and says he'll be out of the larger office by the end of the week."

"He was off on his estimation by a few days." Nic picked up the laptop and tucked it under his arm. "Let's take this back to the house. Maybe you won't have to come in for a few days while we get cleaners in here."

"I don't need taken care of, big brother." From the look I got, I didn't think he believed me.

~

AFTER DINNER, I took the laptop to my room. The good news was I had clothes still in the closet that fit and my desk was stocked with office supplies. It was almost like I'd never left. As the laptop booted up, I grabbed a notebook from my desk.

As Matty had promised, the records were all loaded including a list of the current employees and the records I'd found in the office downstairs. There were also lists of purchases and sales for the last twenty years. Matty had been losing money for a while now. A fact I'd known, but even I hadn't suspected the extent of the red ink. I started making lists of things I needed to follow up on.

A knock came at the door and Annamae stepped inside with a tray. The smell of hot cocoa made me smile.

"I figured you'd be still up working. I made a pot of cocoa and a pot of coffee for you. I made beignets this morning. I was hoping you'd stop by soon." Annamae sat the tray on the desk, then brushed a strand of hair out of my face. "It's good to have you back."

"I'm happy to be here, but I may have made a big mistake buying this antique store." I waved a hand by the computer. "I'm not sure the guy ever made a profit."

"Your brother told me you bought Goldstein's Antiques." Annamae sat down on the bed. She rubbed her fingers. The arthritis she'd fought for years appeared to be winning from the look of her hands. "I attend the same church as Matty's ex-wife. She's always bragging about how much money she gets from him. How successful the store is and even what a complete fool, Matty is. If I had a husband that was giving me the type of money she claims to be getting, I'd be praising the man instead of talking bad about him. But Charlotte Goldstein is all about what's in it for her. I'm surprised she even attends services, but of course, church is the best place to get the newest gossip."

I nodded to the laptop. "She is wrong about the store. It's not doing well. Maybe Matty had some money set aside in his personal account, but if she was getting a large amount of alimony, it wasn't coming from the store. I wonder if he left her in the will?"

Annamae laughed. "It would serve her right to be left out after all the bad things she said about the man. I'm sure she's already called her attorney to see what's coming her way."

Speaking of the Goldstein's reminded me of my aunt. "Annamae, did Aunt Franny ever come visit Grandma Andrews? I mean after the fight?"

The spat between Grandma and Aunt Franny had happened just before my high school graduation. Aunt Franny had sent a card with a check and apologized for not attending the ceremony, claiming to be out of town. But then I'd seen her going into Neiman Marcus the day after. I'd been downtown with my friends, spending some of the cash we'd gotten for graduation and talking about where we were going to school. Most of the girls I'd hung with had gone east to school. I was the only one to go west to Seattle. Even with my choice of colleges, I'd been the outsider.

Annamae shook her head. "Sadly, no. I even called one day to make sure your Aunt Franny knew her mama wasn't doing well. She thanked me, but never came by. I'm sure your grandmother would have loved to see her."

I wasn't so sure of that. And my aunt must have known that what she did couldn't be fixed, at least not with a death bed visit.

"Well, I better get the kitchen cleaned up and head off to bed." Annamae lived in a small house on the property. "I've got a show coming up tonight I like to watch. You just leave the tray in the kitchen and I'll deal with it in the morning."

"Good night and thank you for this." I stood and gave her a hug. The woman was more than just our cook. She'd been there for me after mom had passed and had listened for hours as I talked about the mean kids at school and my plans to go as far away as possible as soon as I could drive. Now, I was back.

"You're most welcome. And I'm so glad that you're back home.

You'll find your place here. You don't worry one minute about it." She patted my face and then left the room.

I went back to the laptop. Before I went through more records, I wrote down Charlotte Goldstein's name. If she hadn't known she wasn't in the will, would she have killed the golden goose? But maybe she was in the will, which even gave her more motive since I'd just made Matty Goldstein a wealthy man.

I mixed the coffee and cocoa half and half into a cup and went back to researching.

Two hours later, both pots were empty and I had a list of questions that didn't make sense. Like for one, why had Sarah been being paid three times more in base salary than most of the other salesman, especially since her actual commissions were few and far between? Mark Bennett, the guy that had been less than friendly when we visited the shop, had a salary almost as large. No wonder Matty hadn't been making money, he was paying out most of his profits in employee costs. Even the most senior designers in Seattle hadn't been making half of what these people were. I needed to do some research on wages for the area before I decided to put out an ad for employees. If this was the normal rate, I'd have to totally revamp my business plan.

I set the cup back on the tray and took it to the kitchen. Then I got ready for bed. Tomorrow would be soon enough to dig more into the dead man's finances.

6

When I went into the dining room for breakfast the next morning, Nic was on his tablet. I poured coffee from the sideboard and grabbed a few slices of banana bread along with an actual banana. Annamae had remembered my favorite breakfast treat. I glanced around the room. "Hey, do we still subscribe to the paper?"

"Annamae has it in the kitchen. I tried to just buy her a tablet, but she said a daily paper was just fine." He studied me. "How much sleep did you get?"

"Enough," I lied. "I'm going into town and working at the store today. I'll stay at the hotel tonight. Thanks for the hospitality."

"You should stay here." But he didn't argue further. Apparently, having Bubba and his friends watching over me eased Nic's worry.

When I got the paper from the kitchen, I went right to the employment ads in the back. From what I could tell, salaries here were in line with what I'd expect to pay in a big city. Cheaper than Seattle, but not what Matty had been shelling out. I folded the help wanted ads and put them into my tote. I finished my breakfast, then I asked Trenton to drive me back into town.

This time the door to Goldstein's Antiques was locked when I used the key. I'd told Sarah that I would call when I was ready to reopened the store. Shutting the door, I relocked it and saw the homeless man from the other day, standing across the street, watching. Waving, I left the front and made my way up the elevator to the third-floor office with the Queen Anne desk. I considered working in Matty's bigger office, but it just felt weird, at least for now. First project, inventory. I printed off the list from Matty's files and found a clipboard in the desk. Then I headed up to the top floor. Might as well work my way down.

By noon I'd cleared only one floor. This project might take days. I stopped at the break room and grabbed a bottle of water out of the fridge. A noise from the hallway startled me. Holding the water out like a weapon, I opened the door to my new office. Nic sat eating a sandwich and playing on his phone.

I let the arm with the water bottle drop and took a deep breath. "How did you get in?"

"You left the door open. I brought you a sandwich." He nodded to the Styrofoam container on the desk. "Eat. I want to talk to you."

"I didn't leave the door unlocked." I glanced down the hallway and thought I'd heard laughter. "What's going on here?"

"I believe they're teasing you." Nic seemed to listen for an answer like the other side was just in the other room. "Apparently they unlocked it to let me inside."

"I think you're the one teasing me." I didn't move from the doorway. "Are you sure you didn't find an extra set of keys?"

"Sleight of hand is a talent." Nic smiled pulled a key ring out of his pocket and tossed it over to my desk. Then took another bite of his sandwich. "These are the keys I took from Sarah."

I went to the desk, put the keys inside my drawer, then opened my lunch. Ham and cheese, my favorite. And a small container of potato salad along with a bag of chips. I unwrapped the sandwich and started eating. I was hungrier than I'd thought. Once the sandwich was gone, I leaned back. "So what's up? Why are you eating takeout with me and not in some fancy restaurant with some business partner?"

"Maybe I wanted to eat lunch with you." When I didn't reply, he continued. "Okay, fine, I found out some things this morning. Did you know that Matty had been losing money on this place when you bought it? Dean might be able to get you out of the deal since Matty died before the three-day waiting period was over."

"I don't want out of the deal. And yes, I knew. But from what I've seen, it's solvable. The sales are here. His expenses were just too high." I focused my attention on the potato salad.

"Our friend Sarah's salary?"

"Among others." I grabbed the notebook from my bag. "Do you know a Mark Bennett?"

"No." He glanced around the room. "If you're going to keep this, and I put emphasis on the word, if, you're going to need better security. Are there even cameras on this place?"

"On my list to check out. Right now, I'm going through the inventory. There are several big-ticket items that should be on the top floor according to the inventory sheet. They aren't there. I haven't had time to look at the other floors, but I didn't find anything additional from the list on the top floor. Once inventory is done, I'm going to have to reach out to Matty's attorney and make sure the items aren't in his house." I finished the potato salad. It had a bit of a kick to it. I looked at the bag when I put the empty container back inside. I'd have to remember this place. "I think I'm going to be here for at least a week verifying the physical inventory list."

"I'll ask Dean to call the attorney." Nic stood and brushed crumbs off his expensive suit. Then he took off the jacket. He called a number on his phone. "Bubba, come on up. We've got a job."

"What are you doing?" I didn't like where this was going.

"Bubba and I are going to help you with your inventory. We might take a little hand holding, but you'll never get done in time if you don't have more hands." He held up a finger. "Hold on a second, I'm calling Dean, He needs to reach out to Goldstein's attorney to make sure nothing leaves that house until we're done with our inventory. We don't want some ex-wife taking off with the property he sold you. It will make things harder to get back."

I hadn't thought of what would happen with Matty's stuff now that he was dead, but Nic was right. I needed to get the inventory done fast, before items I now owned disappeared.

Bubba came into the room. He had several crumbs on his jacket as well, so I assumed Nic had dropped off food with him before he came upstairs. Bubba followed my gaze, blushing as he brushed off the evidence. The reaction made me smile. Maybe there was a heart under all that brawn.

He folded his hands in front of him and waited for Nic to get off the phone with Mr. Dean. When Nic hung up, Bubba asked, "What can I help with?"

"Eddie? Do you want to tell us where to start and what to look for?" Nic threw away his lunch into the trash can by the door.

His action reminded me that I also needed to think about janitorial services and changing the business accounts into my name for the electric and water and trash. With Matty dead, no one was here to cancel them on me, but I still needed to get it done. Having Nic and Bubba helping with inventory would give me the hour to get all that done. At least I didn't need to make a video on how to use the copiers.

I had to admit the truth though, I needed help.

"Okay, here's the plan." I took out the sheets I'd been working on this morning. At least Matty had used a coding system and each piece had a sticker with a code that if you knew how to read it, listed off date acquired and if the piece was part of a set, the number of pieces in the set. "So on the sticker for this table, it should match this code here. 05011999-24-07-01. The date he got the piece, May 1, 1999. It's a seven-piece set and the table is number one. So there should be six chairs to go with it. Like 05011999-24-07-02 He must have bought at least 24 items that day. Like this cabinet, it's coded 05011999-22-00-00. So it wasn't part of a set, but it was bought the same day."

The men looked at me like I had been explaining calculus or some other higher end math. I sighed and looked back at the list. "It doesn't make any sense?"

"All we have to do is look for and match the numbers. Then we can mark it off the list, right? And if it's not there, we can highlight it."

Bubba repeated back his assignment. "One question, what if a piece is not on the list?"

He got it. I smiled and handed him a clipboard showing him the blank paper I'd added to the bottom. "Then just write the code down on this, what floor and area you found it, and a general description of the item. Like table or wall hanging."

"Or really ugly figurine?" Nic added, reaching for a clipboard.

Laughing, I nodded. "You can call it whatever you want, but please try to be specific. Nic, you're on the fourth floor. Bubba, floor two. I'll hit the first floor as soon as I make the calls to keep on the lights."

"Dean says he's filed an injunction on Goldstein's estate, including freezing his financial assets so if you do change your mind, you should still be able to get your money back." Nic said, pausing at the doorway.

"I'm hoping it doesn't come to that. I love this place. You should see all the stuff he has just sitting upstairs. He really needed someone with some design experience working for him instead of paying salesmen way too much with nothing to show for their efforts." I opened the laptop and went to the folder called costs. I should find what I was looking for here. Or at least a starting point. Nic was still standing by the door watching me. "What?"

"You are enjoying yourself, aren't you? I could use you in clearing out some of the locations that aren't making a profit in our family business." He smiled and left the office.

His message was clear. If I decided that cleaning up Goldstein's Antiques wasn't worth my time or that Matty had sold me a failing or dead business, I could go work for the family. It wasn't a job I wanted. But as I made my first call to the power company, it was nice to know I'd be appreciated. And honestly, that I had a fall-back position that wasn't running back to Seattle.

By the end of the day, I had a full list of what was and what wasn't in inventory. I'd check the list against what had been sold the last quarter, but I knew I was missing a lot of stuff. We sat at a table on the main floor, drinking a six pack, and eating tacos that Nic had someone from his office, deliver.

"You have a lot of nice stuff up there. My mom would love to come look at some things for her dining room. She remodeled the house when my brothers and I left home for college. Now that my dad's gone, she's doing it again." Bubba ate another taco and washed it down with a swig of the beer. "This would be a fun place to work at."

Nic shook his head and grinned at me. "You've already brain-washed him to your side. No wonder I can't keep good employees."

Bubba choked on the swig of beer he'd just taken. "Oh, no, I didn't mean I didn't love my job with Ardronic Enterprises. I do. Since you assigned me to watch your sister, I'm a lot more active. Usually, I stand for ten hours a day. Just stand in one place and watch. Which is a good thing, I'm not complaining since it means nothing bad is happening. Maybe I should just shut up now before I talk myself out of a job."

I giggled as I leaned back and looked around at the furniture. "I do have a fun job. That's what I've been trying to tell my brother for years. I'd die if I was stuck sitting at a desk all day. Doing this, I get to be around pretty stuff all the time and make other people's homes beautiful."

"You do seem to have a talent." Nic nodded to the dining room set I'd put up front while I was doing inventory. "Maybe I should hire you to redo the family house. It's been a while since anyone touched anything there. Sometimes it feels more like a shrine to our family history than a home."

"Now that you own it, you can do anything you want." I knew how hard it had been for him to stay behind. To be the one taking care of the family and the business. "If you're serious, I'll take you on as my first client. I can get some great photos and experience that way. And maybe we can have the house highlighted in a local magazine. I'm sure there's a few that would die to get inside our home."

"More than likely," Nic pushed his last taco away, clearly not happy with the idea of more attention. "And now you've ruined my appetite. Let's talk about this place. When will you have a list so we can go to Goldstein's house? The sooner we do this, the more likely it is that you'll get your property back."

"It's Wednesday, right?" When Nic nodded, I continued. "I can match up the missing inventory with the sales records tomorrow."

"I can help." Bubba said, and then added, "and watch your back."

"Okay, with me and Bubba working on it, we should be done tomorrow before five, maybe six." I had kept the lists in front of me and had gone through, highlighting what was missing. The list of misplaced things was really small. Only one or two items per floor. No, the missing items were mostly off site somewhere else. Like Matty's house.

Nic opened another beer for me and handed one to Bubba as well. When he tried to refuse, Nic set the open bottle in front of him. "I'll have someone drive you home when your shift ends, don't worry."

"Thank you, sir." Bubba finished his last taco.

"Anyway, if you can have the list ready by then, I'll have Dean set us up a visit to Goldstein's house first thing Friday morning. Then you can have the weekend to decide if you're keeping this money pit."

Bubba laughed and then covered his mouth. "Sorry, that was a funny movie. My mom used to watch it all the time."

"I'm not changing my mind about the sale. I might ask for some money back to compensate for the missing items." I took in the antiques we were sitting and drinking beer around. Some had come over from Europe with local families whose houses no longer highlighted the beauty of the pieces. Others had been sold in estate sales or when the family fell on hard times. No matter how the pieces had arrived here, they had a story.

You just had to listen to hear it.

A vision swirled around the empty chair next to me. A man in an old fashion suit and wire rimmed glasses smiled at her. "I have to say, I'm quite enjoying listening to you and your thoughts about the items here. You seem to understand the value of things, not like so many of the others who wander past here, looking for the next plastic piece of furniture to waste their money on."

I heard Bubba's gasp but ignored it. If he was going to be hanging around with me, he needed to get used to the appearance of visitors. I focused on the apparition. "I'm assuming you're Harry?"

"Harrold Eugene Winchester at your service. I owned this place a few hundred years ago, it's hard to keep track. Long before Mr. Goldstein bought the place and named it after himself. Such an ego, that man. I called the shop, New Orleans Best Antiques. He thought it sounded commercial. Of course, it's commercial. How do people know what you're selling if you don't announce it." He pointed to the last taco. "Now that smells amazing. What is it called again?"

I explained tacos and their country of origin, at least what I knew about the food. As Harry started to disappear, I realized he might have witnessed Matty's murder. "I'm sorry to bother you, but did you happen to see Matty Goldstein when he was killed?"

Harry nodded, his face sad. But when he opened his mouth, no words came out and the last of his spirit disappeared.

I slapped the table with my open hand. "I should have asked him that earlier. But no, I go on a long explanation of tacos and Mexican cuisine."

"You were talking to a ghost," Bubba said.

"It's a common problem. You get comfortable chatting and forget the most important subject. It's like calling someone and forgetting to ask the one question you called about because you get involved in the conversation." Nic pointed out.

I nodded. "He'll come back. I'll ask him then."

Bubba shook his head and repeated. "You were talking to a ghost."

This time I actually looked at my bodyguard. His face was stark white. "Are you okay, Bubba?"

He took a breath, then a sip from the beer, then a second sip. "I've just never seen a ghost and you just sat there and talked to him like he was a regular person."

"He was a regular person. He just isn't alive like we are." I tried to soften my voice. My grandmother had the same conversation when

I'd caught her sitting and chatting with a ghost in the parlor one afternoon. "It's not scary."

Bubba looked at me like I was crazy. "Ma'am, I've lived in New Orleans all my life and I've never actually seen or heard a ghost. I guess this job is going to be more interesting than I thought it would be when I first took it."

I reached over and covered his hand with mine. "At least you're not just standing for ten hours a day."

He chuckled and let out a breath. "I had to open my mouth, right?"

7

First thing on my list today was an appointment to get the locks changed at the shop. I had no idea who, besides Sarah, had keys. While Bubba and I went through and verified the list of missing items, a locksmith worked on the doors. There were more doors than I'd expected. Two on this floor, the large door in the back on the loading dock had to be rekeyed, and then every floor had two doors. One that led to the stairs, and one that led to an iron fire escape on the back wall. Then there was a door to the roof which was also accessible to the fire escape. The cost of new locks and keys was going to go over my initial budget, but for security reasons, it had to be done.

The locksmith finally finished around noon. Bubba had just called in a delivery order and he was waiting at the front door for our food. I sat at the dining table on the first floor that I'd taken over as my desk. It was easier than working in the office and I could access the collection quicker. The man in the Lost Keys Cause Nightmares t-shirt set a copy of the work order and a ring of five keys on the table.

"There it is. It took longer than I'd expected due to the number of doors in this place. I already gave one to your assistant over there by the door. You've got a lot of real estate here. You should think about remodeling those top floors into apartments. They've got good bones and a lot of space. You'd make a fortune." He keyed some information into his phone while he chatted. "And the good news, that fire escape of yours is solid. That can't be said for a lot of these old buildings. Most of them have had to be replaced by now, but it looks like yours was made strong in the first place.

Harry nodded, sitting beside me. "I put the fire escape in when they first came out. Maryann wanted to go with the less expensive, but I insisted on putting in the best. You can't be too safe, right?"

I pressed my lips together, trying not to react to Harry's statement. I turned away from him and toward the locksmith. I glanced at his shirt for his name. "Thanks Leo. I appreciate your thoroughness. Since I just bought the place, I have no idea how many keys are out there."

"It's a smart idea to replace the locks. One of my other clients bought a shop that had a lot of old jewelry. He decided not to replace the locks, trusting that the prior owner had given up all the keys. He was robbed within a week. Then he puts new locks on. Kind of like shutting the barn door after the horse escapes. Anyway, you did the smart thing, even if the price tag is a little higher than normal."

"Do I pay you?" I glanced at the scribbled numbers. They looked like product code, not prices. Kind of like the coding system Matty had set up.

"No, the office will send you a bill. They said I didn't even need to get a deposit. Apparently, you have good credit with us." He looked around the room. "You got a lot of nice things in here. You might want to upgrade your security system while you're at it. We don't do that but we have a referral I can give you."

While he dug in his bag for the security company information, I leaned back and closed my eyes. What had I been thinking? I should have started with something smaller. Like that Garden District shop Danielle had shown me. Something that didn't have five floors and needed a lot of upkeep.

"But then you wouldn't have me to help out," Harry said to my left.

I opened my eyes and looked at him. I didn't realize ghosts could read minds.

Harry laughed, "Even if I couldn't read your mind, your face tells the entire story. Buck up, buttercup. Things will be okay. I've got faith in you."

The locksmith had a flyer in his hand and was watching me. Apparently, I'd missed something he'd said. "Sorry, I was just thinking about the security system."

"These guys are solid. They're not going to blow smoke at you or over charge. Tell them that Leo sent you and they'll even give you a few bucks off the final deal. The guy that runs it is my cousin's brother-in-law. He has horrible tastes in football teams and politics, but other than that, he's a pretty good guy." Leo set the flyer down and looked around again. "The one good thing about this place is it stays cool. No matter where I went, there seemed to be a chill around me. A lot of these old buildings are hotter than hades. Sorry for the swear word."

I thanked him and walked him out of the building. On the way, I met Bubba who had our food. He gave me the food, then took Leo to the front door so he could relock it. I set the food down on the table and glanced over at Harry who was still hovering. "I take it you followed him around this morning?"

"Yes. You never know what type of man they're going to send. He's one of the good ones. He admired some of the items but took great care with his work tools and didn't break anything. You should give him a positive review with his employer when you pay them." Harry leaned into the table. "What's for lunch?"

"Today, it's a taste of New Orleans. I ordered a little bit of every-thing, just in case you were picky." Bubba answered Harry's question as he set the key on the table. "He gave me this, but I thought you might want it."

I held up the ring. "I think I'm good. You can have it while you're working with me. That way if I get a call in the middle of the night about something going on with the building, I can send you and go back to sleep."

"Like that would happen. You'd be down here before I could even get my shoes on. You're pretty hands on with this business." He blushed and started taking food out of the bag. "I ordered a red fish dish, shrimp and grits, beans and rice, gumbo, and some shrimp jambalaya. And creole bread."

"That's a lot of food." I took in the smell and almost melted. Harry seemed to be in his own food coma.

"I thought we could share and eat family style, unless you want something specific." Bubba looked at the dining table covered with food. "Maybe I went overboard."

"Maybe a little, but it's great." My phone buzzed with a text. "And look who just showed up. Can you let Nic in? I guess there will be three for lunch."

Harry watched as Bubba hurried to the front door. "That man's a keeper. You're lucky."

I stared at Harry's softly disappearing form. "Bubba is my body-guard, not my boyfriend."

He hovered over the shrimp and grits, taking an exaggerated sniff. Then he looked at me before he disappeared. "Does he know that?"

"Hey, sis," Nic stopped a few feet away from the table. "Wow. I came over to see if you needed lunch, but I guess that's already been handled. Were you hungry?"

I stood and gave Nic a hug. "I'll have you know that I didn't order this feast. Bubba was kind enough to order for us."

Nic held up his hand. "Way to go, bro."

The men did their bonding slap and I sat back down. "Harry was here for a bit but I didn't ask him about Matty. He looked so happy about the food, I didn't have the heart to bring it up."

"You can ask him next time." Nic sat at the table and grabbed a plate. "Speaking of our late antique dealer, I've got us an appointment to go through the house tomorrow at 8:00 AM. The judge wants this part of the discussion done and over with so he can schedule a meeting with the creditors. Apparently, the ex-wife is pushing for a speedy will reading."

"Annamae knows her." I took the red fish dish and put some on my plate with the sauce. Then I grabbed the rice and beans. "She's not her favorite person."

Nic chuckled. "I've heard that from a lot of people. Anyway, will you have the list ready?"

"If I have to stay here all night, I'll have the list done." I took a bite and groaned in pleasure. There was nothing like the seasonings they used here in New Orleans. I could have almost the same meal delivered in Seattle, but it would have either been served with no sauce and limited spices to highlight the fish or with an Asian flare. Every place had their own mix of what food should taste like. And this, this was like being home. I broke open a roll and took a bite without butter. It was sweet and fresh and before I knew it, the roll was gone.

Nic looked up from his plate. "Eddie, I thought you'd be closer to being done. What have you been doing all day?"

"One, it's only lunch time. And two, we have new locks and a lead on a security system upgrade. I know the alarm system Matty set up is still active, but I'd feel better about hiring my own company." I reached for the jambalaya. "Besides, I was kidding. We should have this done by five or six at the latest. Just like I'd said yesterday. Bubba's getting really good at identifying different historic periods."

Bubba nodded. "My mom would be proud. She wanted me to do something creative with my life, but I went practical at college and got a business degree. Between that and football, there wasn't a lot of time for extra classes."

A noise sounded from the front door. I stood up and saw Aunt Franny banging on the glass door. She looked mad. "This can't be good."

"I can tell her to go away," Bubba stood and moved toward the front.

"No, I'll go. Nic, you stay here as well. No need getting us both in trouble." I walked over and unlocked the door, but only opened it a few inches. I could feel Nic and Bubba watching me. "Hey, Aunt Franny. Sorry, we're not quite open yet. I can give you a call when we are."

"You spent my money on this firetrap? Are you kidding?" She

glared at me. Then she started shaking her finger like I was a five-year-old child. "That money was supposed to go to me. I'm her daughter. I'm supposed to have her powers."

"You're going to need to take that up with Grandma." I leaned against the doorframe. I wasn't going to tell Aunt Franny I knew about the love potion or about the fight. That was between her and Grandma. "Now, is there anything else? I've got work to do."

"If you don't relinquish the money and the power, I'm going to cut you off. You will no longer be my niece." Her gaze was cold, calculating.

I had no doubt she would do it. I remembered Saturdays at the house. Grandma, Mom, and Aunt Franny cooking in the kitchen, getting everything ready for a family get together. Now all but Aunt Franny, Nic, and I were gone and she was threatening to cut off communication over money? Or was it the power my grandmother had passed on to me that she was really after. Either way, it wasn't my gift to give back. "Grandma made her choice. I can't change it."

"But you can. All you have to do sweetheart is a small ceremony. Your blood to my hand. It's simple." Aunt Franny smiled and softened her voice. She stepped forward reaching out for me.

I dodged her grip. "You're misunderstanding what I'm saying. I won't go against what Grandma had set up. You had your chance to fix your relationship while she was alive. I was out of state. I didn't even know you two were fighting. I didn't do this. You did. If that means you're also going to cut me off? I can't change that. And, I won't. It's your choice. You know where I'll be if you change your mind."

I shut and locked the door in her face.

She beat on the glass with both hands, furious at me. For a second, it didn't even look like the aunt I knew standing out there. I felt a presence next to me. I looked over and saw Harry watching me from a wing back chair.

"Sometimes doing the right thing is also the hardest thing to do." He smiled at me then disappeared again.

I took one more look at the aunt who'd promised to never talk to me again and went back to the others. My food was getting cold.

Nic and Bubba watched me as I walked back to the table. I sat down and picked up my fork. "Apparently, Aunt Franny won't be at family holidays unless I'm not invited."

Nic reached out and covered my hand with his. "Sis, you'll always be invited. She'll come around eventually."

I blinked back tears. "She let Grandma die without making things right. Or even trying. I have a feeling that I won't be seeing Aunt Franny again."

We finished our meal in silence, then Nic made a call. He came back and started throwing empty containers into a trash sack. "What can I do to help?"

"With the audit?" I knew he didn't mean Aunt Franny. That situation was between her and me. She'd made her choices. Family is hard.

He broke the last roll in half and offered half to me. "Yes, with the audit. We're expected there first thing in the morning and I'm not going to let Franny's visit change our plans."

I took the roll and nodded. "Let's get to work then."

WITH NIC ON BOARD, it took less time than I'd expected. I got into the restaurant in the hotel, Criollo, for an early dinner. Bubba had refused my offer to feed him so he was standing by the wall, watching. It made me uncomfortable to always have security around me. Another reason I had moved away from home as an adult. I'd talk to Nic the next time I saw him and have him pull Bubba. Or at least reduce it to when I was out of the hotel. This was ridiculous.

I had just finished a great meal off with a dessert, coffee, and a little time with a book when my phone rang. Even across the room, I could see Bubba's change in stance. I pulled it out of my tote and answered, "Eddie Cayce."

"Ms. Cayce, this is Detective Boone Charles. We met a few days ago?"

I smiled and I saw Bubba relax across the room. "Yes, Detective Charles, I remember. What can I help you with tonight? Did you find Matty's killer?"

"I'm sorry to have to disappoint you on that front. We're still investigating. But since your shop was the murder scene, I've been watching it for any unusual activity. A beat cop chased off an attempted break in just a few minutes ago. I don't know if you want to come down and check your locks or security, but I'll be here for about another thirty minutes if you do."

I had stood up and waved at my server as soon as he said the words 'break in'. "I'll be right there."

I signed for the meal, then met Bubba at the door to the lobby.

He took my arm and moved me through the crowd. "What's wrong?"

"Someone tried to break into the shop. The police are there now." I pointed to the door. "It will be faster to walk than try to get the car out."

He activated his earpiece, calling someone. "The princess is on the move. We'll be at the antique shop at time of transfer."

I didn't stop walking, but I glanced up at him. "You call me the princess?"

"Sorry, that name was set before I knew you. Your brother's code name is prince. Your dad set them up years ago." He smiled down at me. "Although sometimes you do look like a princess."

"If I had time, I'd show you who looks like a princess." I paused at the corner, waiting for a car to move past before crossing without the light. I could already see the flashing lights in front of the shop. "I can't believe what a mess moving home has been. It's one thing after another."

"You're just settling in. I hate to say it, but this won't be the last time someone tries to break into your shop. We're in a high tourist area. Drunk tourists can make bad decisions. Especially around spring break." He held his hand up for an oncoming car and hurried me back onto the sidewalk.

"Thanks for the positive spin on this." We had one more road to cross and a crowd of people to get through before we were there. I took a deep breath as we approached the building. No windows were broken from what I could see. I hoped I was right. If there had been, I'd need to get someone in to board it up until I could get the glass replaced. Detective Charles waved me over to where he was talking to a homeless man.

When I got closer, I realized it was the same man I'd seen around the store the last few days.

Detective Charles nodded to the man. "Tell Ms. Cayce what you just told me."

The man glared at the detective but nodded. "He tried to use a key but it didn't work. Then he started yelling and had a crowbar. I thought he was going to break the window, so I started yelling at him and waving my arms, hoping he'd go away. A crowd of people stopped and one guy started filming. I don't like my picture taken, so I turned my face. He saw the camera and went running. Then a cop showed up and said I was trying to break in. I wasn't. Find the camera man."

He was getting agitated. "Calm down, I believe you. Did you know the man with the key?"

Detective Charles frowned at me. Apparently, he didn't believe the man's story.

"He comes a lot. Or he did, when Matty was here. He wasn't nice like Matty. He told me he'd call the cops and have me arrested. I didn't let him see me after that. Matty was nice." Tears fell from the man's face. "I miss Matty. When you see him, tell him Kirk says hi."

No one had told him that Matty was dead. I looked up at Detective Charles and he shook his head. I started to dig in my tote, but Bubba anticipated my need and handed me a ten. I gave it to Kirk. "Thank you for your help tonight, Kirk. I appreciate how you watch the place."

"Payday is coming. Matty pays every Friday morning." His eyes brightened when he took the ten. "Kirk will be back then."

As he started to leave, Detective Charles reached out to stop him, but I grabbed his arm. After Kirk was out of sight, I turned back to him. "He didn't do this. He's around all the time. If he wanted to break in, he had a lot of opportunity. He was helping Matty."

"I think you're right, but why would someone with a key try to break in?" He took off his cap and wiped his face with a handkerchief.

"Because I changed the locks today. If someone had a key, it's from before I bought the place." I went over and looked at the new lock. A key had been dropped on the ground next to the door but behind a planter. I pointed it out to the detective. "Detective Charles? Any chance you might get a fingerprint from that?"

He came and picked up the key with a tissue, then put it in a small evidence bag. He held it up to the beat cop who now stood next to Bubba. "I guess we assumed that we had our suspect a little too soon."

I nodded to the doorhandle. "You'll need to fingerprint that too, right? Can you check to make sure it's locked? I'm wiped and would like to go home."

"I'm calling the crime techs down now. Go home and get some sleep. I'll check it as soon as they dust it for fingerprints. Can you get me a list of all of Matty's employees? I think we need to look a little closer at some of them." He glanced over to Bubba. "You have an escort? Or should I send one of my guys?"

"I have a shadow." I stepped away from the detective. "Thank you and I'll send you that list tomorrow to your email. I still have your card."

As we walked back to the hotel, Bubba got a call. "We're on our way back now. I'll meet you in the lobby."

"Your replacement is here?" I asked as we weaved through the crowd. Someone was drinking a Hurricane and I could smell the fruit juice as we walked by.

"He is." Bubba moved us around a crowd of drunk college kids talking about where to go next. "I'll be here in the morning to go with you to Matty's house. I'm not scheduled on until noon, but I adjusted my hours so you didn't have to have someone new there."

"That was nice of you." I figured Bubba actually wanted to be part of what he saw as a scavenger hunt for the missing antiques. "I'm having a drink when we get back. Do you want to join me?"

He shook his head. "I won't be on duty then. My replacement..."

I paused at the door to the hotel. "I wasn't asking you as my bodyguard. I owe you for all the work you did on the missing items. Come and have one drink with me. Then I'll let you get home to your wife or girlfriend. I just hate sitting alone at a bar. Men think you're lonely."

He laughed at that and nodded. "I can have one drink before I head home. Fluffy won't mind."

"Your wife's name is fluffy?" I pushed the door open and headed to the bar. I could see that there were still seats on the rotating carousel with the circus animal stools. If we hurried, I could snag a lion.

"Fluffy is my cat. I don't have a wife," he paused as they settled onto seats at the circular bar, "or a girlfriend."

8

Friday morning, Nic waited outside the hotel in his limo. Apparently, he wanted to make a statement when we hit Matty's neighborhood. I slid inside and Bubba followed me.

"Coffee?" Nic offered as he held out a carafe. Annamae sent me with some banana bread and a question on when you're coming over to the house again. She misses you."

"I know. I need to come out more often. Maybe after we get the shop up and running. Did you hear about the attempted break in?" I sank into the seat and reached the carafe.

Nic nodded. "Trenton monitors the police channel. You should have called me last night."

"I was fine. Bubba came with me to the shop." I refilled my coffee cup and screwed the lid on tight. I didn't need coffee spilling all over me or Nic's leather seats because we hit a bump.

"Oh, I thought this happened later in the evening. Did your replacement not arrive?" Now Nic's gaze was focused on Bubba who had just turned a bright shade of red.

"No, sir. I mean, yes, Terry came on time, but this was when the princess, I mean, Ms. Cayce was eating dinner." He blushed and kept talking. "Then after we returned to the hotel, I stayed and had a drink with Ms. Cayce."

Now, Nic wasn't looking at Bubba, he was watching me. "Interesting."

"I was technically off the clock." Bubba continued.

I reached out and touched Bubba's arm. "You didn't do anything wrong. He's just messing with you."

Relief filled Bubba's face as he looked back and forth from Nic to me. Something in our faces must have told him he wasn't losing his job, at least not today. I sipped my coffee, thinking about last night's events. "I'm beginning to think that one of Matty's employees had something to do with his death. This place was a goose with golden eggs to some of the employees. They were making double what they should have been paid, and if you take into consideration the commission, it's triple. Whoever tried to get in last night had to have been after more of the antiques. We need to find most of these things in Matty's house so we can stop looking over our shoulders."

"What did Detective Charles say?" Nic handed me a slice of banana bread, then two slices to Bubba.

"Not much. At first, he thought it was Kirk, the homeless guy who has been hanging around the shop. Then I found a key that the guy had tried to use, that matched Kirk's story, so he asked for a list of Matty's employees. I'm sending it to him today after we finish up with Matty's house."

"Charles said he was thinking about charging the homeless guy?" Nic leaned back in his seat, watching my reaction.

"Kirk, his name is Kirk, didn't do it. He loved Matty and he doesn't know he's dead. I'm going to have to tell him somehow, but I'd hate to send him into a tailspin. He's coming by today for his paycheck. I'll talk to him then."

Nic choked on the swig of coffee he'd just taken. "His paycheck? This homeless...I mean, Kirk is on your payroll? This is the reason I moved my businesses out of the French Quarter. Too many panhandlers."

"He's a nice guy in a bad spot. We all have issues."

Nic watched me for a bit, not responding. Then he shook his head. "You've always had a soft spot for the losers in the world. Just make sure that someone's with you when you talk to this guy. Okay?"

"I'm beginning to feel like I'm five and heading off to kindergarten." Nic's eyes flared so I backed down. I wasn't going to win this fight. "I'll be smart and have one of my bodyguards with me."

Trenton turned the limo onto a side street and the houses got even bigger, a feat I didn't think possible in the Garden District. "It's up here on the left, sir, but there's a car in the driveway.

I watched out the window as we pulled into the circular driveway and behind a small convertible. The top was down and showed the cream leather interior and the bright yellow paint job. I suspected it was a BMW, but it could have been something else. I wasn't that good with identifying car makes. Especially since I hadn't owned a vehicle in Seattle at all. I'd lived close to my office and if I went somewhere, I'd ordered an Uber or walked.

A woman got out of the car and put her hands on her hips. "It's about time you showed up. I've been waiting for over an hour."

We climbed out of the limo, including Trenton who'd turned the car off and was holding his cellphone, just in case.

"And who are you, exactly?" Nic asked as we lined up in front of her.

"I'm Mrs. Mathew Goldstein, and I'm the owner of this house." She brushed the fur from her coat away from her face. She'd been running the air to enable her to keep the coat on without suffocating in the already muggy day, but now that she was standing outside the car, she was melting fast.

"I didn't think Matty's will had been probated yet." Nic walked to the front door. "We have permission from the court to be here, so if you'd excuse yourself, I'd appreciate it."

"I drove all the way here at the crack of dawn today. You're not going to keep me out of the house while you three steal me blind." She stepped on the sidewalk in front of Nic.

"You're not going to keep me from doing what I need to do. We're not letting you inside the house." Nic tried to step around her, but she blocked him. He looked back at Trenton. "Do you mind?"

"Not at all sir." Trenton picked the woman up by her arms and moved her off the sidewalk, giving us room to get around her. She sputtered but didn't fight him. "I'll keep the trash off the sidewalk while you go inside."

"You can't call me trash. I'll get my money from Matty, even if I have to dig his body up to get him to sign a new will." She yelled at us as we headed into the porch held up by three Grecian columns. The house seemed to chuckle at the scene.

Nic took a key out of his pocket and unlocked the door. When we were in the cool foyer, Nic turned to me. "Well, our Annamae wasn't too far off. The woman thinks she's getting all of Matty's stuff. Speaking of delusional people, have you heard from Aunt Franny again?"

I shook my head. I didn't want to talk about my aunt and her lack of family ties. "Money, it changes everything. I never thought she'd say the things she did."

Nic leaned closer, checking to see if Bubba was out of earshot. "It's not just the money for our aunt."

"I know, but this isn't quite the bonus power most people dream of when they want to be superheroes." I studied the vase on the table. Taking my list and clipboard out of my tote, I handed a sticky pad and pen to Bubba along with a clipboard and list for him and did the same for Nic. "There's one of my items. Put a star on the stickie and see if you can find the number on the list. I think it's Ming dynasty. Maybe about halfway down the list. There's a picture of the item next to it. Then take a picture. I hired movers to be here at ten, just in case we found the items."

"Always thinking ahead., I can give the judge the list and the pictures of what we took out of the house." Nic nodded to the baby grand in the next room. "Is that on the list? I was looking for one on the second floor a few days ago."

"Good eye." I scanned the list. "Number forty-two. Put the

number on the stickie and mark it off your list. Everyone take a room. Hopefully we'll be close to done before the movers get here."

We spent the next few hours, reclaiming items that Matty had 'stored' at his house. If the ex-Mrs. Goldstein was still watching, she'd be furious at the amount of things we took out of the house. But even then, there were still several missing items still on my list that were worth a lot of money. As we waited for the movers to finish loading their truck, I sat in the foyer, marking up my list with the finds that Nic and Bubba had found. "I wonder if Matty had a second house?"

"Not according to the judge. He sold it a few years ago. Maybe some of these items were in there and he just didn't remove them from inventory?" Nic took a drink of water. "Give me a second list showing the still missing items, I'll take it to the judge and put a hold on anything that looks like what we're missing." He jerked his head toward the door. "Or maybe he'll give us a warrant to check her place too. She seems the type to help herself."

"Is she the type to kill her golden goose?" I looked out the window and saw her standing by her car, yelling to someone on her phone.

"What, you think she killed Matty?" Now Nic watched her as well.

"I think it's worth a question to Detective Charles to see if the grieving ex-wife had an alibi. Did the judge reveal who Matty's heirs were? Please tell me it's not her."

"According to the judge, but not to be discussed elsewhere, the ex-Mrs. Goldstein is going to be very disappointed in her inheritance. Matty's lawyer told me that Matty said she'd drained him for years when he was alive so when he died, he didn't have to hear her complain." Nic nodded to the window. "The ex-Mrs. must have a salon appointment because she's leaving."

"Or her lawyer told her to get out of here before it looked bad to the judge." Bubba said as he walked back into the foyer. "I just checked the garage and the outside sheds. Nothing that looked like what could be on your list. He does have a nice cherry red 65 Mustang convertible I'd give my right arm to own."

"Good thinking to check the outbuildings." I stood and looked around. "Did we check the basement and attic too? Matty was a hoarder, at least with antiques."

"I checked the attic and Bubba volunteered to do the basement. No missing items in either." Nic opened the door for the movers. "We deserve lunch for this."

I checked items off the list as each time the movers left the house to take something to the truck. They handed me the stickers on their way out. "And that's the last one that's here. The movers will be at the shop in thirty minutes or so. I need to be there to let them in. The joy of owning your own business."

"I run a business and I get to eat lunch," Nic commented. He held up his hand to stop my next remark. "I'll send Trenton to get us food after he drops us off at the shop. We'll probably have to eat after the movers finish. Do you have room in the loading area for all this?"

"This and more. Bubba and I moved around things yesterday to make sure it was cleared." I tucked my lists into my tote. "I'm not sure what I'm going to do without your help, Bubba. Maybe I need to actually hire some employees."

Nic held the door open for me and we stepped from the cool air-conditioned house into the muggy heat. And it was still technically morning. I missed my Seattle weather. Just not the job or the ex-boyfriend.

"Are you sure you can't keep on any of Matty's crew? Hiring is hard right now. I hate you to have to hire an all new staff." Nic waited for Bubba to step onto the porch and then locked the door. He pocketed the key.

"I can't afford to pay them what Matty was paying and stay afloat. So unless they want to work for a standard wage, I won't be bringing them back. And, with all this stock missing? I'm a little skeptical that some of it isn't in their homes. If Matty did it, maybe it was a common practice." I smiled as Trenton opened the back door of the limo. "Thanks, Trenton. You must have been bored out here. We should have brought you in on our scavenger hunt."

He shook his head. "Your brother asked me to watch the woman and the other car. When she left, I read. I always carry a book, just in case. I enjoy thrillers."

I climbed in the car and as I waited for the other two to get inside, I dialed Detective Charles. I guess I was more of a mystery type. At least in real life. "Hey, thanks for picking up. I have a question."

"With as big of a butt as I felt yesterday about blaming that homeless guy for the break in, I thought I should answer so you could dress me down for my assumptions."

"I think your beat cop led you down that path. It's okay, I get it. But that's not why I'm calling. Did you run the ex-Mrs. Goldstein's alibi? Any way that she's our killer? Matty just came into a lot of money, maybe she needed an influx into her personal accounts?" I saw Bubba grin at me. I ignored him.

"She was our first and best suspect. The only problem was she was out of town the night Matty was killed. At a spa getting a weight loss treatment. At least that's how they described it to me when I called to verify. They had a private nurse with her all night since the treatment can be a little intense on the digestive system. If you get what I'm saying."

I shuddered. I definitely didn't want to lose a few pounds at that cost. "Okay, but she could have hired someone. Set herself up for an alibi."

"True. And that's why she's not off the list, I'm just not seeing any paper trail or money exchanging hands. I still need the employee records. Can you get those to me today? Or do I need to stop by the shop. I know you're busy getting ready to open."

"I'm just leaving Matty's house and I'll be in the shop in, twenty..." I looked at Trenton to confirm and he waved his hand back and forth, indicated around twenty. "Make that thirty minutes. I've got to work with the movers but then I can email it to you or you can come get it."

"Email it to me to the address on my card. I'm a little swamped in paperwork today."

I dug into my tote to check and came up with the card. "I'm sorry I've taken so long. I'll get this to you as soon as I get back and into my office."

"No worries. I should have used it as an excuse to come see you today, but like I said, I'm swamped with follow ups on Matty's murder."

I wasn't sure how to respond to that. Or what it meant. I took a breath and assumed he was just being friendly. "I'm sure I'll see you soon, anyway. Thanks."

After I hung up and put my phone away, I realized both Nic and Bubba were staring at me. "Oh, he says that the ex-wife has an alibi, but she's still on the list. He needs the employee list as soon as possible, so don't let me forget to send that when I get back."

Nic smiled and leaned back. "He seems chummy with you. Are you sure there isn't something else going on?"

I felt my brow furrow. My mom had always yelled at me to stop letting my emotions show on my face. *It's going to freeze that way or worse, cause lines making you look older.* I think it was just my normal reaction to Nic's teasing. "He's investigating Matty's murder. That's all."

Nic laughed. "If you say so."

I watched as Bubba turned his head and looked out the window. What had I said wrong now?

9

When we got to the shop, Kirk was out front, pacing. His face lit up when he saw me.

"Matty hasn't come to pay me yet. Can you call him?" He held out his dirty hands. I didn't think he even noticed the action.

"Oh, Kirk, I'm so sorry. I'll pay you today for Matty. I had somewhere else to be this morning and I forgot. How much was Matty paying you for security?"

Nic cleared his throat but I shook my head, hoping he wouldn't interrupt. Kirk was skittish, especially after last night's incident.

"Fifty dollars a week. Four ten-dollar bills, ten one-dollar bills. Not too much so I'd be attacked, but I can pay my locker rent and still have money to buy food." He kept his hands out.

I didn't have that much in my wallet, but as I dug, Bubba held the money out to me. I glanced up at him.

"I'll put it on my expense sheet."

I took the money, then counted it out for Kirk. As I did, I thought about what he actually needed. A place to stay. "Maybe I can find you a room to stay in as part of your rent."

He frowned at me. "I don't go to shelters. They need those beds for the people with families."

His words broke my heart. He was sleeping on the sidewalk to keep the bed at the shelter for a kid? I nodded. "Actually, I was thinking about something here in the building. So you'd be close if anything happened, like last night."

Nic touched my arm. I knew what he wanted to say, but to his credit, he let it go.

"Anyway, let me see what I can do. I'm reviewing all the employees to make sure we're paying market rate, so getting you a room might just be enough to keep me from paying you so much money and then you have to figure out how to keep it safe." It was all a big lie, but if it kept Kirk from feeling like I was offering charity, so be it.

Kirk nodded. "We can talk about it. I have to go. The soup kitchen opens soon."

We watched him hurry away. Then I opened the lock to the shop and locked it after the men had followed me inside.

"You're getting rid of all of Matty's employees because you don't trust them. But you're keeping the homeless guy who sleeps in your doorway?" Nic adjusted the closed sign.

"Your point?" If Nic told me it was too dangerous or that I didn't know this guy well enough to give him a room, I'd point out the fact that he stopped someone from breaking in last night.

"You're pretty amazing, sis." He turned toward Bubba. "Let's go watch for the movers."

I went upstairs and found the employee list. I printed it off, then sent a copy to Detective Charles. Then I took the list back downstairs to our worktable. Maybe there was someone on Matty's payroll that wasn't making a ton and could be trusted.

Using the payroll records, I matched up all the names and what they were being paid. When I was done, Nic and Bubba were back from helping the movers and Trenton had brought our lunch. My stomach growled at the smell of the pizza. "I'm starving."

"Me too." Nic opened the boxes and put a couple of slices of an everything pizza on a plate, handing it to me. "How's the employee search going?"

"There's a few weird things. One, there are way too many employees for this size of store. Even if Matty was open six days a week, and from the sign on the front, he wasn't, he didn't need fifteen salespeople." I counted the number of employees on the list. "One manager and one business office manager, but fifteen salespeople."

Nic picked up the list. "A lot of these addresses are close. Maybe we should go and tell them about Matty's passing. The funeral is this weekend, right?"

"Yeah, but isn't it mean to say your boss is dead and you're out of a job?" I took a bite of the pizza. "But on the other hand, if they invite me in to see if I'm keeping them on at the shop, maybe we can find some of the missing items. Or mark people off as suspects."

"There's a flaw in your plan. Just because they don't show the pieces in their apartments, doesn't mean they didn't steal and sell them." Nic pointed out.

I conceded the point. "I bet they'd keep some and showcase them. If you love working in an antique store, you love nice things. You couldn't help yourself."

Bubba raised his hand. I laughed and waved at him to talk. "Don't you think it's weird they haven't shown up? I mean, you had that one lady the first day you came who was working, but since that time, no one has tried to come in to work. Unless you count the guy using his key last night. And he came after shop hours."

Nic and I stared at him.

"What? Did I say something stupid?" Bubba looked back and forth from me to Nic.

"No. You said something really smart. Unless Sarah called all the employees and told them about Matty's death, they should have shown up for their shifts. Or called. But it's been radio silence." I glanced down at the list again. "Several of these people don't have a cell phone listed. Actually, none of the salespeople besides Sarah, who is really a manager, and this Mark Bennett have phone numbers in the system. There's a number for Matty and the business office manager. But no one else."

"Let's go see if we can find these people." Nic finished the last bite of pizza on his plate.

The first fourteen addresses were bogus. No apartment available or if there was, the tenant that answered the door told us they didn't know the person attached to the address, or Matty. They *had* heard about the antique store changing hands. Several asked when we were opening.

Now I knew how Matty was losing money. He'd been paying people who didn't exist. I wondered if he'd known about the issue. Or if this was someone else's scheme? We might never know, but I was going to call Detective Charles tonight and see if he ran into similar results.

Nic glanced at the list. "Well, we're down to Sarah and this Mark Bennett. We know Sarah knows about Matty's death." He keyed the address into his phone. "Mark lives just a few blocks from here. Do you want to pay him a visit?"

"According to the schedule, he mostly works weekends." I held out the hope that maybe he just hadn't heard about Matty's death.

"Which is a good reason to visit." He pointed toward the next cross street. "It's that way."

They walked two blocks farther into the quarter, then turned left down a one-way street. Nic leaned close and glanced behind us. "We're being followed."

"I know. It's just Kirk. He's been behind us since we left the shop." I didn't turn back since I could see the guy's reflection in the glass window of the restaurant as I walked past. "He's harmless."

"I'll tell the police that when they are investigating your death in that rat trap of a building." Nic pointed to an arched entryway with an iron gate. "Mark lives in that building. Upstairs, in 201."

We stepped into the entryway which led to an interior courtyard with a fountain. The temperature dropped and I could feel the coolness that the water added to the air. Sarah Stiner sat at one of the tables. When she heard our footsteps, she wiped her eyes, then hurried past us, not speaking. I turned to go after her, but Nic held me back.

"One problem at a time. Let's see why she was here talking to Mark."

We walked up the narrow stairway and went down the open hallway to the door with 201 on the front. Nic knocked and the door was thrown open.

"I told you to leave me alone. It's not my fault you didn't take care of your own future..." A small man in a Nike t-shirt with a scruff of beard stared out at them. The small living room behind him appeared to be furnished in priceless antiques from the area I could see. "Sorry, I thought you were..."

I stared at a lion bust on his foyer table, number five on the missing list, and interrupted him. "You thought we were Sarah? Why was she here?"

Mark ran his hand through his thinning hair. "She's upset about what happened to Matty. Can you blame her? We worked together for over five years. We're more than just co-workers."

"Are you lovers?" Nic leaned against the doorway, looking way more casual than I knew he felt.

"What? No. We were friends." He paused and I could see the wheels turning in his head. "I guess it doesn't matter now, but our friend Sarah was in love with the boss. It was hard to watch, her being so head over heels and him being totally oblivious."

"So they weren't a couple? It was all one sided?" I watched his face for reactions.

"Who knows. I don't get into other people's business." He glanced back into the small living room. "Look, I'm job hunting so unless you're here to tell me I'm one of the ones you're keeping on, I need to end this conversation."

"So you know who I am. I'm having some issues finding your coworkers. Do you have any update on them?" I figured Sarah must have delivered the news. "And, can you tell me why you were being paid twice or more salary that's normal for your position?"

A smile curved his lips. "You are into the details, aren't you?"

When I didn't respond, Mark shrugged. "What can I say, Matty was generous to a fault. And I'm really, really good at what I do."

Nic took my arm. "I suspect you are. Let's go. There's nothing here."

"What's that supposed to mean?" Mark curled his fist and stepped closer.

Bubba stepped in the space between Mark and Nic. "I don't think you want to do that."

I could see the discussion going on in Mark's head before he dropped his arm and uncurled his fingers. He hadn't seen Bubba standing there. Now, he didn't like his odds. He grabbed the door. "Just leave. There's nothing more I want to say to you."

As we made our way out to the street, no one spoke. We were almost back to the shop on Royal when Nic mumbled, "He's hiding something."

"You mean beside the fact he has at least one if not more of the missing antiques from the shop in his apartment?" I stopped walking, grabbed my notebook out of my tote. "Let me write down what I saw so we can check it against the inventory list. Then I'll call Detective Charles again."

Nic paced on the sidewalk, waiting for me to finish. "I don't believe she was just there to grieve. She's part of this."

I tucked the notebook back into my tote. "You think Sarah killed Matty? Or Sarah and Mark killed him?"

"I think either scenario is a good bet. Of course, there's no proof." Nic sighed and leaned up against the wall. "You need to keep yourself safe. I'm not feeling good about this situation."

"I knew Matty was gone." A voice to my right side said, "Check the video."

I saw Kirk standing by the corner watching us. "Did you say something?"

"Matty installed cameras. He knew there was something wrong

with the store. He hired me to watch at night, but I didn't see anything." Kirk shook his head. "I must have fallen asleep. Stupid, stupid."

"There are cameras inside the store?" I took a step toward him which was the wrong thing to do. He ran out into traffic.

"Stupid me, stupid me." He chanted as car horns blared as he darted in between two cars.

After Kirk got safely across the street, I met Nic's gaze. "Let's go find these cameras."

It took us a while to find the closet where Matty Goldstein had set up the rest of the security system. Four televisions were showing the main show room, the outside, the back door, Matty's office, and the conference room. Nic glanced at the system. "I don't want to mess with this. Call your friend the detective."

Detective Charles showed up in less than thirty minutes with a bunch of officers. He and his officers huddled in the closet for several minutes. Then he and the others left with the tapes. He told me he'd be back after chatting with a few people. Four hours later, just Detective Charles returned to the shop. While we waited, I matched the list of everything that was supposed to still be in inventory that I'd seen in Mark's apartment. I handed him a copy of the list. "If Mark didn't kill Matty, he was at least stealing from him. All of these items should still be on the show room floor."

"We'll let you go through the apartment as soon as crime scene gets done with it. It might take a while for you to get everything back, but at least you'll have a full list." He nodded to the cups on the table. "Mind if I have some coffee? I think it's going to be a long night. And thanks for checking out most of our list. You saved me a ton of time."

Nic nodded to a chair at the table. "Have a seat. I'll get the coffee. So do you think Mark's the killer?"

"Killer and thief apparently. I got a call from the station a few minutes ago. Sarah Stiner came in and confessed to cooking the books. Her story is that Mark told her he was going to kill the old man, but she didn't believe him. Until it happened."

"I don't understand, why would she confess?" I watched as the detective sipped his coffee.

"Now that's the weird part. Stiner said Harry told her she had to confess if she wanted to sleep at night." Detective Charles watched as we exchanged glances. "Do either of you know who Harry is? I'd like to talk to him."

10

I decided to move out of the hotel and back into the family compound a few days after Harry pushed Sarah into doing the right thing. Nic hired me to redecorate and update the house. It's hard taking a fresh eye to the home where we grew up together, but on the other hand, after being away for a while, it feels like a fresh canvas. And having a paying project gives me time to hire staff at the store since Matty's prior employees were facing charges. At least the real ones.

Well, except one. With Bubba's help, I've updated an apartment for Kirk in the building. I talked to a social worker who had been keeping an eye out on him for awhile and Mrs. Cameron assured me that Kirk wasn't violent. He'd come home from a war and didn't fit into his family life anymore. So he left. And then his issues got worse.

Someone had built an apartment years ago on the first floor at the back of the building. Maybe it had been for the shop owner or a maintenance man. It was perfect for Kirk. It has a door directly to the alley. He has a place bigger than a locker to store his things and an actual bed to sleep in. Nic brought over a television and a recliner and updated the kitchen appliances. Kirk should be fine, but I'll check in with him from time to time. After all, at least today, he's my only real employee.

Even with me moving home, Nic's insisted on keeping my body-guard nearby, so Bubba's been helping me with the remodel. It's above and beyond his 'job duties' but he seems to be having fun. Today I'm reviewing the job applications that have come in with the hiring service. And drinking coffee in the kitchen with Annamae.

A knock on the kitchen door marks Bubba's arrival, but today, he's not alone. An older woman with short grey hair cut in a bob and bright blue eyes follows him into the kitchen. I closed my laptop.

"Eddie Cayce, this is my mom, Heather King. Mom, this is my boss, Ms. Cayce. Mom would like to talk to you about one of your sales openings." He took the cup of coffee Annamae had gotten up to give to him. "If this is a bad time, she can come back."

"Call me Eddie. It's not a bad time at all," I stood and reached out my hand. "It's nice to meet you, Mrs. King. Your son has been a life-saver here, not just as my security guy, he really has an eye for design as well. Have a seat. Can I get you some coffee?"

"Call me Heather, and I'd love some coffee."

Annamae had already poured a cup and set it in front of Heather. "Cream or sugar? These two like it black but we can serve it however you'd like."

"Black is fine with me. I like to taste my coffee." She smiled at Annamae. "Thank you so much."

"Tell me about you. I know you raised a strong and polite son, so you've already got my attention." I turned a page in my notebook and wrote down her name and Bubba's mom under it.

"Beauregard always was a joy and a delight. He was an Eagle Scout at fifteen. Of course, I bribed him and said if he didn't get his Eagle, he couldn't take drivers ed until he was seventeen." She tucked her Kate Spade purse on her lap and put her hands on the table, touching the coffee cup, but not taking a drink.

"I didn't know that" I said, then my eyes widened. I turned to Bubba whose face was beet red. "Wait, your name is Beauregard?"

"Don't even. There's a reason I've always gone by Bubba even though it makes me sound like I have a fourth-grade education, instead of being a college graduate." He sipped his coffee. "And Mom, this interview is about you, not a walk down memory lane for my childhood. So no mention of Peggy Sue Majors or the time I broke the toilet tank cover."

I laughed and turned back to Heather. "He's right, of course. I need to know more about you, but now I'm really curious."

"We'll do coffee one day without my private son," Heather promised. She handed me a small notebook. "I went to college for design, but when I met Beauregard's father, I became a stay-at-home wife and mother. My job was to keep the house and throw parties, at least until I had a child. I kept up with the design trends and remodeled the house often. My husband indulged me with whatever I wanted, except having outside employment. Hank's been gone now about two years and I've been puttering around that big house by myself for too long. I've brought pictures of the house and the redesigns I did over the years. I was a frequent customer of Goldstein Antiques and Matty kept me on his new inventory list So I'm aware of what you have in stock. Or I was."

I opened the notebook while she was talking. Her first page was a resume, mostly highlighting her college experience but also she had taken several classes through the years in different subjects, including New Orleans history and even some art history classes. Then I turned the pages and got lost in the pictures. She'd done an amazing job of taking a space and making it pop. I could tell the areas she designed for entertaining and the more family areas. I smiled when I saw what must have been Bubba's or maybe one of his brothers' bedroom change over the years from a nursery, to a baseball themed kids room, to a teen's room, and then more of generic male bedroom, but with family touches. Like a bat and ball she'd put in a memory box with his uniform. I looked up and smiled.

"I can bring more pictures if you need them. I also helped several of my friends redecorate over the years." She twisted the cup in her hand. She still hadn't taken a sip.

"There's no need. This is just what I need. It won't just be a sales

job. I plan on providing design services for local residents as well. If
we have what they need, that's great, but we'll be shopping the other
stores for items as well as suggesting new furniture when appropri-
ate." I'd been thinking about what I wanted to highlight with my
business for several weeks now that I owned the antiques store. "I
don't just want to be known as a pricey antique store. I want us to
help make people happy in their homes."

"It sounds perfect. I wouldn't need much of a salary. I was well
taken care of in the estate." Heather rattled on.

I saw Bubba close his eyes. He was thinking the same thing I was;
Heather was horrible at negotiating. It was her first job interview
from what she'd told me. I smiled at him when he looked over at me,
trying to convey that I wasn't going to screw over his mom. "Heather,
if I hire you, I'll pay you what you're worth. And you should never
expect less."

Her face went blank for a second. Then she nodded and sipped
her coffee for the first time. "I guess you can tell I'm a little nervous.
Honestly, I really want the job. Beau, I mean, Bubba has been telling
me what you're doing and frankly, I'm a little jealous. I can do a good
job for you, I promise. Even without a work history."

"Well, that's all I can ask for, right?" I closed my notebook and
stood. "You're hired. I'll have to get all the paperwork at the shop so
we'll meet there tomorrow at eight. We'll talk about money, benefits,
and hours then. I'd like to open the shop at least for appointments
only in the next week or so. But let me show you our first project."

She stood and dropped her purse on the floor, forgetting it was
sitting on her lap. "Seriously? I'm hired? You don't need background
checks or references?"

"You have a reference sitting here. Bubba wouldn't have brought
you to meet me if he didn't think you could do it." I waited for her to
get her purse. "Do you have a notebook in there? Or a phone to take
pictures of the rooms?"

After Heather left for the day, I went out to the front porch to
review more applications. One employee was amazing. Two would be
better. And if I wanted to have some regular open hours, I needed at

least four. And a CPA or a business office manager. I had a lot to do if I wanted Goldstein Antiques up and going by the end of the month.

Bubba came up and set a glass of sweet tea on my table. Then he leaned against the railing watching me. "Thank you for taking her seriously. She's been trying to get up the nerve to come talk to you for the last week. She's redone that notebook's pictures at least three times."

"Your bedroom was cute." I sipped my tea, watching him. "And she's the perfect employee, even without a work history. She's just what I needed. Do you have any friends in the same boat?"

"Actually, that was Bobby's bedroom. Mine was football themed." He laughed and shook his head. "I don't know anyone who loves design like my mom. But I'm sure she might have some referrals if you ask her."

"I'll do that tomorrow." Setting the glass down, I exhaled. "I've got a long list of things to do and I keep adding to it. Opening this business is going to take a while."

"All you have to do is what you can do right now. Don't worry about everything but keep putting things on your list to get better. That's what my dad always said. You don't have to be perfect today, but you need to do the work to be better tomorrow."

I watched a blue jay land on the tree near the porch. "I like that motto. I might steal it."

He studied me for a long minute. "After Nic reassigns me, I'd like to talk with you about something."

"You want to come work with me and your mom?" I teased watching his face for indicators of what the subject might be.

He shook his head and stood up. "I have a job. We'll talk later. I'm going to walk the perimeter, unless you need something."

"No, I'm good." I watched for a while as he stepped off the porch and went around the west side of the house. My mind pressed on the question, what did he want to talk about? I could only think of one thing, he wanted to ask me out on a date. My stomach clenched a little as I thought about the way he looked in that suit. And the way his bright blue eyes watched me. Was I ready for a relationship after breaking up with David? Probably not, but I could be ready for coffee.

And that's all I needed today. Or whenever Beauregard King stopped being my bodyguard. I was ready for coffee.

I sipped my tea and went back to finding a few people to interview tomorrow. My new life in New Orleans was beginning to pull together. I'd lost my grandmother, and Aunt Franny, at least for now, but I'd gained something I hadn't known I'd been looking for. A place to call home.

A chuckle came from the wicker couch on the other side of the deck, but when I looked over, my grandmother was disappearing. "I love you Grandma. Thanks for bringing me back home."

A faint, "You're welcome," echoed on the deck, then the sound, like her apparition was gone as well.

Time to get to work.

READY FOR MORE?

Want more Lynn Cahoon cozy mysteries? Check out my website at www.lynncahoon.com and sign up for my newsletter to stay up on the fun.

A MEDIUM HOMECOMING – A Haunted Life cozy mystery - Book 2 – releases December 6, 2022 and is available for pre-order at - My Book

Eddie Cayce had come home to New Orleans. Good or bad, she's made her bed and now she has to sleep in it, like her mama always said. The trouble was even though she loved the town she grew up in, the gift she'd been given from her late grandmother was causing problems. Major problems.

Her aunt wasn't talking to her. And her ability to talk to ghosts has been turned up to the equivalent of a million-watt light bulb. Walking down the street from her newly purchased antique store, she has to dodge questions and demands from the newly and not so dearly departed.

But when her marketing associate, Tessa Hunt, dies unexpectedly, then shows up on Eddie's doorstep demanding that Eddie find the killer, she's stuck between a rock and a hard place. Especially since Tessa keeps pushing her bad marketing tactics from beyond the grave.

All Eddie wants is a little peace and quiet so she can run her new business and find the perfect house. Is that too much to ask? Apparently, the answer is yes, at least in New Orleans.

LEGAL BITS

Made in United States
Orlando, FL
24 August 2022

21495271R00055